COSPLAYED

Laura Maisano

Rayha studios

Lake Dallas, TX
www.RayhaStudios.com

~ For Keely, Louis, and all my cosplay friends who inspired my geekdom

to take literary form ~

COSPLAYED

Laura Maisano

Audrey

If smell could kill, I'd have died long ago. Early Saturday morning the "con funk" had infiltrated the dealers' room like a critical hit on a ballroom-wide Cone of Stench. Unwashed bodies packed between the tables managed to produce an odor ripe enough to have its own name. Gross, über gross, but strangely enough con funk comforted me. I dunno, maybe like how IcyHot conjured memories of Grandpa. The dealers' room was like home.

My booth blended in with all the others. A few ruffled tablecloths, oversized graphic banners, and collapsible wire racks transformed six-by-four folding tables into miniature storefronts. A guy sporting a Naruto headband handed me a box from my table—an unopened Darth Vader figure, vintage.

"Forty-five dollars and sixty-eight cents," I said.

"Better than eBay." He flicked out his Mastercard, and I swiped it through the machine. It beeped, stopped, and I swiped again. The old ticker-tape thing finally spat out a receipt. Uncle Rick really needed to upgrade to something made this millennium. Maybe Dad could convince him. They'd been best friends since high school, so Dad might have a shot.

I ripped the yellowed receipt and pinned it under a pen on the clipboard. "Sign here."

We finished the fumbling dance of transaction. Dude took his generic plastic bag filled with 1970s swag and shuffled into the mob. Attendees hunted through the packed aisles for treasure while I watched, hoping to make a buck. Uncle Rick could use more than a few bucks. Maybe then he could afford an iPad or an inventory system more advanced than me counting on my fingers.

The crowd parted, and three Power Rangers rushed the table almost knocking down my merch. I stumbled over a crate.

"Hey! Careful." I twisted my foot behind the boxes to find a spot to stand.

"Audrey," said a muffled voice inside the Red Ranger helmet.

"Dan?"

He yanked off the homemade helmet. Sweat plastered Dan's scraggly locks to his forehead. "Yeah. Remember Cora and Jake?" He pointed behind him at the yellow and green rangers with his thumb. "We really need your help."

"Oh no. No." I felt their stares through my hoodie, trying to measure me. "I don't cosplay. I'm a dealer."

"Jessica got sick last night, and her costume is finished. Please? We prerecorded the voices, and it wouldn't make sense without the Pink Ranger."

"I told you before. I don't dress up." Even the extra-large T-shirt branded with the *Infinity Games & Comics* logo drew too much attention, like a sideways figure eight pointing at my non-chest—mocking me.

Dan leaned in, pouting. "Pleeeeeease?" Another driblet of sweat dropped off his chin and onto a laminated sign, which read *Dollar Comics*.

"Stop sweating on the inventory." I nudged his spandex-covered arm away from the table.

"We've worked." Something inaudible mumbled inside Cora's helmet. "Months…have to…"

Green Ranger nodded behind her, agreeing with whatever else she meant to say through the layers of plastic and modeling clay.

The curtain brushed my ankles, and Uncle Rick ducked into the booth, his arms loaded with more UFO dolls for the display. "Go. Have fun with your friends tonight."

"That's okay. You need me here to man the booth." Saturday was prime selling time. He needed sales—really needed the sales. And I wanted an excuse.

Dan shook his head. "Dealers' room closes an hour before the contest."

"One hour isn't enough time to practice."

Uncle Rick set each of the dolls in a line on the rack. "You can leave 'round five. The crowd slows up when the big panels start, you know that."

My throat tightened, and I grabbed the edges of my hoodie, crisscrossing it over my front. "But—"

"Don't worry, hun. I've got it covered." Uncle Rick fixed the crooked corner on the poster behind him. "You love this stuff as much as I do. 'Bout time you took a chance to enjoy a con, instead of watching from behind a table."

Behind the table was safe. No one noticed the invisible hand giving change and sliding credit cards. Watching was fine with me.

Dan got on one knee, knocking over a set of bobble-heads on the way down. "Help us Audrey Warren. You're our only hope."

"Where's your adorable beeping droid?" I puckered my lips to keep from laughing.

"Is that a yes?"

"I'll head to the room five-ish. Now, let the paying customers by, will ya?"

Dan popped his helmet on to cover an outrageous grin. Then he said something, but all I heard was "regret it." He probably said something like I "wouldn't regret it," not that I believed him.

I zipped my oversized hoodie closed. How'd he know? I'm pretty sure the Red Ranger was some Japanese guy in a suit, not a psychic.

The Hilton bathrooms left much to be desired in the way of space. When two people crammed in the sink area jamming themselves into spandex bodysuits, the tiny room could barely contain the jumble of flailing limbs and swearwords.

Cora helped tie my hair into a knot at the nape of my neck. The loose bits pricked behind my ears, tickling like a bug trapped inside. I'd go crazy for sure. This whole thing was crazy. Letting a friend of a friend help me dress in skin-tight spandex added to the level of insanity. Did she think Jessica should be here instead? The costume wasn't mine. Did it look right?

In the mirror, my reflection blinked back at me. Bright pink—neon day-glow Pepto pink on steroids—covered me from head to toe. "Why'd I agree to this?"

"You did great at practice. You'll do fine." Cora slicked her black bangs with gel.

"I didn't mean that. The part is easy, nod along to some dialogue and fall down." I wrapped my arms around the white belt at my waist. The stupid costume was skin tight. "I meant wearing this. I feel…exposed."

Cora bent and grabbed my helmet from the edge of the tub. "No one will even know it's you or what you really look like." She pushed the pink bug-eyed thing into my arms. "Pretend you're the Pink Ranger if that helps. You have a secret identity. It's a costume. Have fun with it."

I pressed the helmet to my chest, like my own kind of barrier. Maybe she was right. No one could see into the visor, and I didn't take it off in the skit. As long as I wore the mask, I was safe.

Before I felt ready, which would have been never, Dan herded us from of the room into the lobby of the convention center. The con drew in people of all walks of life—an older couple in matching shirts which read *I love you* and *I know*, a family dressed as Pokémon trainers with the kids as Pikachu and Squirtle, all the way down to packs of teenagers hoisting "free hugs" signs. But more than anything, the cosplayers came out to shine, especially Saturday night. Some single cosplayers wore elaborate getups, carrying props made movie-set realistic, and others worked in groups like ours. Those singles must be brave.

"Oh dude! Check out the Power Rangers group." A guy in one of those packs pointed at me or, I guess, us.

His friend dug into a cargo pocket. "Awesome costumes." He wrangled out a camera. "Can I get a picture?"

I turned to the others, my motion exaggerated by the bulky helmet. They had already moved to face the camera.

"Sure!" Dan yelled through his mask.

Cora pushed me between her and Jake. I stood there like a tree, a confused, anxious tree with shaking leaves. *They're all doing poses. Should I pose?*

Jake elbowed me. "You saw the show. Just pretend you're her."

"Okay, on three!" The guy fiddled with a button on his camera.

One.

I didn't have time. I had to do something.

Two.

I balled my hand in a fist and pretended to punch the air in front of me.

Three! Flash.

Another flash, and I struck another pose. The others did the same, acting just as ridiculous as the Rangers in the show. It didn't matter what we did; it couldn't look sillier than the real poses.

The first guy with the camera left, but another replaced him right away. Then another group approached, cameras and phones out and ready. We kept striking poses, arms above our heads. I did a fist pump, lunged sideways, and reached for the sky. Bizarre contortion? You name it, I did it. Our group didn't even have to move. People kept coming to us. More flashes, more pictures, more poses, and hidden inside the helmet, I smiled.

Behind the curtain, I stood in a sardine pack of cosplayers, crushed between Dan and Cora. Jake was somewhere under my left elbow. Stale air recirculated around my face. I breathed the suffocating CO_2 faster. If they didn't announce the awards soon, my precious helmet would end up killing me. I might pass out anyway. Then I wouldn't have to face them.

Getting on stage had been a mistake. I shouldn't have entered the contest knowing how my body liked to go to freak-out mode. Lights, sounds, everything had jumbled together. Missing my cue had been bad enough, but then the awful fake fall played in my head again. I jumped too far, hitting Cora, and we collapsed like crayon-bright dominoes. Why didn't they have a hole around here somewhere I could crawl into? A black hole.

The speakers crackled. "Okay everybody, the judges have tallied their votes, counted the points, and made their choices. Let's get the awards rolling."

Someone jabbed me in the shoulder with a gunblade as the excited crowd backstage attempted applause.

"This is it." Jake retrieved his helmet from between his feet. If we won something, he'd want to show off his face to the audience. Good for him.

Dan kept his helmet on, so I couldn't decipher whatever he said.

The announcer grabbed a handful of envelopes from the judges' table. "First award, funniest skit goes to." Pause for dramatic effect. "Final, Final, no really, *Final* Fantasy."

The winners shuffled past us and leapt up the stairs to the stage to thunderous applause. Jake mumbled, "There goes our one shot."

Right. After the whole disaster, comedy would've been our only reprieve. I put my hands on the sides of my helmet. I held it tighter.

More winners joined the judges on stage. They walked past me, each wearing the most unbelievable costumes. Honorable mention was a group named Zombie Wonderland, the Cheshire Cat alone could give me nightmares for a week, followed by an Alien Xenomorph, and someone with a ball gown glowing with LEDs.

The costumes all bore the marks of passion—details. They were crafted with care, down to the Alien's sculpted veins and the petticoat for the gown. I had stopped hyperventilating, but their creativity stole my breath.

The announcer paused for a drumroll sound effect to end. "First runner up is Apocalypse and Magneto from X-Men!"

"Second place...we deserved first." Apocalypse grumbled, wrinkling his prosthetic makeup. Jogging to the stairs, his ultra-wide shoulders banged into my helmet, and he hopped onto the stage without apology. Magneto followed close behind.

At last, the announcer raised the final envelope above his head. "And Best in Show goes to..." He tore it open. "Optimus Prime!"

The rest of the winners congratulated the guy in the huge armor getup, and while the audience applauded, the other contestants began to regroup. Some already filed through the door in the temporary wall that'd lead them out into the convention area. Dan and Cora took off their helmets, looking like they wanted to do a postmortem on the contest.

Not me. Not now.

I hurried in front of a group of exiting cosplayers to get away from the others and snuck through the door.

Audrey

Sunday morning flashed by, and at four o'clock, Uncle Rick had me packing up the booth. As a truck backed into the loading dock, the obnoxious beeps weaved into the rest of the cacophony. Wire racks collapsed, vendors shouted orders to each other, and everyone forgot how to move without knocking down crap in the loudest possible way.

I placed a stack of Dungeon Crawler books into a crate, added a box of dice, and then Uncle Rick dropped in a mess of loose buttons.

"This crate's for roleplaying stuff. I labeled it." I snagged a plastic bag and shoveled in the buttons.

He tossed the bag back into the crate. "We'll sort it at the store. Just get everything packed for the truck."

Ungh, that wastes so much time. And no, *he* wouldn't organize it at the store. *I'd* organize it at the store, just like I'd do every Friday night from the previous week's don't-worry-about-it attitude. Though he wasn't blood related, he could irk me on a level that rivaled my sister. Sometimes more.

"Hey!" Dan emerged from behind a pallet stacked with tables. "Need any help?"

"Did your dad say you had to tear down?" I snapped the crate closed, with the stowaway buttons still inside.

"No, I'm not technically an employee, but I thought I should help out, too."

"Uh sure." I reached under the table and slid another crate between us. "Load this one with comics."

Uncle Rick called from behind the curtain. "Pack fast. Just dump it in."

I shook my head, and Dan winked at me. At least we'd load one crate the way it was labeled. For the next minute, we dropped merch into the box in silence. I glanced at Dan. Guilt kneaded my stomach like dough. My fingers locked onto a stack of comics, and I slowly released it into the box. Did he blame me for losing the contest last night? I disappeared right after, too. Was he mad?

"Did you have fun yesterday?" Dan asked.

I caught a breath in my throat. "What?"

"Did you have fun?"

The contest itself was the definition of nightmare—spotlights, loud music, a gazillion people staring at my crash landing. After all the talk about the skit not making sense without me, it sure as heck didn't make sense *with* me either.

"I'm sorry." I focused on stacking another handful of comics. If I didn't see his disappointment, maybe it'd sting less.

"For what?"

I lifted my face. His eyebrows twisted in confusion. "You lost the contest 'cuz I messed up," I said.

Dan burst out laughing so hard he had to wipe his eyes. "Really? No, Aud, we probably didn't have a shot to start with. There were some epic skits, and no way would the Power Ranger costumes get one of the craftsmanship prizes. We entered for fun." He locked the lid on the crate. "Cora and Jake are theater nuts, so they can't give up a chance to perform."

"They're not mad either?"

He bopped me on the forehead with a plush Pokémon. "No one's mad." He repeated, "But, did you have *fun*?"

"Well, not the contest. That…I'm not doing that again." I stood, adjusting the edge of my shirt, the black tent I cowered under. But yesterday, a bright, outrageous costume freed me from some self-imposed prison. People took my picture while I acted like a dork. It felt amazing.

"You were right." I grabbed Dan's arm to help him stand. "I had fun in costume. And don't say 'I told you so,' okay?"

"I told you so."

I wound back to take a swing at his arm, but he ducked. "I just said—"

Dan razzed.

Though he acted like an annoying little brother, I was lucky to have Dan and his family. My sister, Sara, wouldn't be caught dead at a con. If she knew I had done the whole "dress-up thing," she'd probably die from embarrassment for sharing the same DNA. She wasn't always like that, though. When we were little, Sara would've been the one to shove me on stage for a dance recital…wouldn't have been much different. But she'd changed. Had I changed, too?

A loud *snap* shook me from my daydream as Uncle Rick unhooked the first of the wire racks. The curtain collapsed to the floor. "Are all the crates packed?"

"Almost," I said.

Dan grabbed the last box and tossed a pile of stuff inside. "Gonna cosplay again?"

No, of course not, you insane? That's what I meant to say, but that flutter in my chest returned at the thought of those cameras, the playacting, the thrill. I'd caught the bug, but admitting it to Dan would mean conceding defeat. I wouldn't lie either, just to have it bite me in the butt.

I grabbed the last lid and snapped it on his crate. "Maybe."

Maybe…definitely.

For the next couple of cons, I borrowed a handful of Jessica's old costumes—Spider Gwen, a princess Teenage Mutant Ninja Turtle mashup (complete with tutu skirt), and her stormtrooper gear. All of which had masks or helmets, of course. It was restricting to rifle through a selection of someone else's stuff, and really, that little cosplay bug had grown. I'd contracted a full-on infection, and if I put something together myself, I could choose *anything*.

Endless possibilities.

After school on my day off, I drove all the way to the Denton mall. The place was so small it even had one of those brow-shaping businesses and a store that sold "Cell Fone" accessories, but the lameness meant it could also house one of the largest costume supply shops around. They sold dancewear too, probably where they got all the real income. I'd asked Sara to meet me there since she went to college nearby, which was probably a silly excuse. I wanted to hang out with my sister, and since she left for school, there hadn't been many opportunities. Or opportunities she took advantage of.

While I waited, I scoped out the store for ideas. Prepackaged costumes packed the walls and filled free-standing racks, which made narrow aisles. Huge garment hangers took up the center of the store with rental costumes, many of which were leftovers from local community theaters, and they ranged the gamut from generic medieval to characters from the latest movies. Glass cases were filled with makeup, beads, elf ears, spirit gum, gloves, accessories, and all the knickknacks that the craft stores didn't carry. Sequins, capes, wigs, petticoats, corsets, and—holy crap—a whole display of full-body spandex suits in an array of colors and designs. My brain zoomed at a thousand thoughts per second. I could make anything I wanted.

Someone poked me on the shoulder. "Wait long?" Sara asked as I turned around. She swept me into a hug, squeezed, and released.

I wobbled back into balance. "You're just in time."

She reached and tugged the collar of my T-shirt, straightening it then smoothing the shoulders of my hoodie. "There, all set. You're not working, you don't need to wear the sweatshirt."

My hands began to brush more wrinkles out without asking them. "It's like my skin now. I can't take it off or everyone will see my true alien flesh."

"Can't let that happen, can we." She snickered. "Okay alien-girl, I do need a new leotard, but why'd you want to meet here? What's the big secret?"

With an exaggerated flourish, I gestured at the racks of costumes. "I need your opinion on a cosplay. I want to get something new, but it's hard to pick what would look good on me."

Sara's pouty lips half-smiled, then she glanced around. "Sure. Uh, okay."

"Thanks, Sis."

Her little smile broadened, and she hooked an arm behind my shoulders. "Lead the way."

We walked a zigzagging path between racks as I put different things together in my mind. What about an anime-inspired cosplay? Most of those didn't have masks, though.

Sara pointed at the back wall. "Nineteen-twenties' burlesque totally screams your name. It's sparkly teal, too. Your favorite color."

"There's a pink one next to it. We could be twinsies."

Her bubbly laugh led to a hiccup, so she held her breath. Mixed with her glare, the air-filled cheeks made her look like an angry chipmunk. She exhaled and razzed me at the same time.

"I know, you won't dress up. But for real, I want a new costume. Help me out." I bumped into her with my side, and she nodded, appearing to look *seriously* at the costumes.

Though I don't know why I asked. She wouldn't know what to look for, really. To the left, a Batgirl cape caught my eye. I could do her, a female Riddler, or they even sold stuff for a femme Flash. I took the Batgirl costume off the peg; good quality rubber for the mask even. "What do you think?"

"Pretty classic, I guess." She chuckled. "Even I know who that is, so you'd be recognized."

"That's true. DC just isn't as cool as Marvel, though." But few of the Marvel costumes had the secret identity part nailed down so well, at least for the girl characters.

Sara shoved me with her elbow. "You're such a nerd." She pulled out her phone and put her head on my shoulder. "Do your best duck face."

Duck face really wasn't my thing—it was a Sara thing…a cheerleader slash dancer slash cool-girl thing—but I smiled for the selfie. She tapped the phone a few more times, and the *zip-ding* meant she'd uploaded it. She shared a picture of me. Had she sent it to her new friends? Or maybe she just posted to her Instagram, but either way the big smile I had stretched wider. Why was I surprised? We were sisters. Of course she'd share selfies of us together.

I lifted the costume off the rack. "Okay, I'll try it on. You can get your leotard while I get dressed."

She nodded, and I grabbed a backup size before heading for the changing room. A clerk counted the items and unlocked one of the little wooden stalls, and I tossed the extra costume onto the bench along the back wall. It had enough room to move, but no mirror. I squeezed into the bodysuit. Medium fit on the bottom, but was loose on top. Maybe it looked okay. Grabbing the mask, I left the stall to check it out in the mirror on the wall. The costume sagged a touch. What if I sewed up the sides?

"Sara, what do you think?" I turned around, peering through the narrow mask.

She was holding a leotard, preoccupied with her phone. The beeps of the messenger app tinged loudly in the quiet store, one after another. *Ping, ping, ping.* Someone was chatty.

"Hey!" I called again.

Startled like an animal, she popped her head up from the phone. "Oh, sorry." She hurried over. "Great, looks great. You should get it. I'm gonna check out."

"We just got here."

Ping, ping.

"Oh, hey. I know. Take another selfie with me. Your friends will love the costume." I moved next to her, and she leaned away.

"It's low on battery." She dropped the phone into her purse. "I've got to hurry. They're almost here."

"They're in the mall?" I deflated from the inside out, like my helium high got sucked away and left a party-balloon husk. We were supposed to spend the afternoon together, us. Just us. We had so little overlapping time these days.

Sara hoisted her purse onto her shoulder and gripped the hanger of the leotard in the other hand. "Yeah."

So much for sister time. At least I could meet her new friends and we could all hang out. They had to be better than Sara's old high school clique. You had to be smart to go to college. "Wait a sec. I'll change quick."

As if on cue, five girls of the trendy variety approached the wide opening of the store where it met the hallway of the mall. Sara bolted to meet them, and as she paid for her item, they formed a circle around her, like a sun with its orbiting planets. Her new college friends fit the type, though graduating high school had transformed them from cheerleaders to dancers. Was that even a thing?

Though, they came here knowing Sara and I were spending the day together. Sara had shared the picture of us, so they knew she was with me. I had to hurry to keep up. More like the Flash than Batgirl, I changed with super-human speed and ran out to meet them at the entrance of the store. The empty entrance. Even the cashier had abandoned the till and resumed hanging packages of tights.

Of course. Of course they were gone.

In two huge strides, I sped back into the dressing room where I could scrunch my face and suck back the tears in solitude. Stupid, stupid, stupid. Why'd I think Sara had changed? Why'd I think she'd want me to meet her friends? I knew I'd never be a part of her world, one of the worshiping planets, but something inside wanted her to claim me.

Audrey

After the run-in with Sara's posse, I returned home without the Batgirl costume, and instead brought back a valuable lesson. Sara wouldn't post a picture of me as long as I wore a costume, mask or no mask. She'd assumed her friends wouldn't like a little geeklet like me. If someone was an ass, they'd be an ass. And I probably wouldn't find too many at a con. After all, con-goers all liked the same stuff I did. United by fandom, or something.

From then on, I wouldn't let a lack of face covering keep me from cosplaying something new. This time I'd get to play the character I really wanted. Before the next big convention, I commissioned someone on Etsy for a costume and ordered a wig off eBay. I kept the costume hidden the whole way to the convention hotel. Dan had begged me to tell him the character, but I let him writhe in the suspense as I changed in the bathroom.

"Hurry up, I want to seeeeee," Dan whined outside the door.

At least this hotel had more space to work with. The double sink area gave twice as much elbow room. "Almost done."

I removed the lid from the hat box on the vanity. Slow and gentle, as if handling a priceless tiara, I lifted a yellow wig. Four-foot ponytails unfurled to hang on both sides, each connected to a powerful sphere of a bun. Before, I used to curse my thin brown hair, but it flattened to my head to fit easily inside the cap, slipping into another persona.

The face in the mirror vaguely resembled me, since I never wore such dramatic makeup or yellow-blonde hair. I winked at my reflection, and the character came to life. I giggled. She giggled.

A fluffy red bow connected to the sailor collar on my front. Another bow fastened at the small of my back over a blue skirt. Add that to the white leotard, and people could mistake me for a Lady America if they didn't know better.

"Audrey, come on." Foot tapping accompanied Dan's sigh.

"Okay, okay." I slid open the door and struck a pose, my white, gloved fingers in a peace sign next to my face. Picture perfect.

Dan covered his mouth. "Sailor Moon?" His gaze moved up and down. "I don't think your skirt is screen accurate."

I yanked at the slippery hem, pulling it down even further. "So what, I prefer modesty over accuracy." I shoved past him into the hotel room. "Jerk."

He shouldn't be looking at my skirt length anyway. The boy grew up down the road, and I'd known him my whole life. Maybe that's why he thought he had the right to comment.

"And you're like a cousin. Don't make weird comments," I said.

Dan held his hands in surrender. "Hey, hey, sorry. It looks great, awesome really. I was kidding." He added, "And I'm *not* your cousin. My dad's not *really* your uncle, ya know. He's your boss."

"Yeah, yeah." I paused. "I'm not sure I want to do this now. Maybe I'll go back down to work." I hugged my middle, the white spandex between the big bow over my little chest and the *apparently* inaccurate skirt. I thought it covered enough. I was wrong. Maybe I should put on a mask or something.

Dan spun me toward the gigantic mirror above the dresser. "You look just like her. I was joking, okay?"

The girl in the mirror looked insecure and scared. Sailor Moon grew out of that, didn't she? That's why I chose her. She cried a lot and sometimes tried to run away, but when she transformed into Sailor Moon, she learned to be confident.

I switched back into my role, put on the smile, and tried to be someone better than me. Did it work? Would everyone see right through?

"Come on, I'll walk you to the convention center. Someone's gotta cover your shift at the booth," Dan said.

"I thought you weren't 'technically' an employee?"

He opened the door and waved me out. "Yeah, but then Dad mentioned that the store buys me food, so I receive salary by proxy."

"Nice." I followed him into the hall. The A/C blew cold against my exposed legs, but I didn't care. Sailor Moon didn't care.

Once downstairs in the hotel lobby, a group of girls—including two Disney Princesses—ran toward us.

Ariel dropped her bag. "Holy cow, Sailor Moon. That's awesome!"

"I love your costume."

"So cool, can I have a picture?" One of the girls rifled through her backpack in a hurry as if she was afraid I wouldn't stay long enough.

"Uh, sure." I glanced at Dan.

He nodded. "I'll head back to the dealers' room. Have fun being a star." He continued on through packed convention center toward the ballroom.

The enthusiastic fans whipped out their phones, and I struck a new pose, with a peace sign of course. In the moment, I let go of my fears, and the silly part of me emerged like I'd uncaged a monkey on pixie stix. Sailor Moon giggled openly, smiled, and talked to strangers like friends. I could too. I did.

As soon as the girls left, another couple came with cameras out and ready.

Flash! Flash!

More people asked for photos, and I obliged. Amateur photographers appeared one after another in a ceaseless pattern of stop, pose, and *flash*. The more that came, the further I delved into my act.

I spun in a circle, pretending to throw my tiara. "Moon tiara action!"

The couple taking pictures at the time laughed and smiled with me. "Do the other attack. The one with the moon wand!"

"Sure." I held my fist as if I had the real prop and lifted my leg in the air while mimicking the contortions that anime Sailor Moon was capable of. "Moon healing…uh…escalation!"

Another group stopped to watch, huge smiles on every face, but none bigger than mine. My smile, my face, not the character. Even Sailor Moon couldn't have this much fun. I kept popping exaggerated poses, waiting for the next camera flash. Soon enough, my feet protested in their heeled boots. A dull ache formed in my arches, stretching up the calves. It went on like that for an hour before traffic died down.

Finally, an opening.

I hurried around the corner and found a lull in the insanity of the con floor, an empty bench by a trash can. That wall didn't lead to any rooms that had programming going on, which allowed a bubble of space to form wide enough to see carpet without having to look through hundreds of legs. Practically limping, I claimed the bench and took a deep breath. I'd never dreamt that posing for pictures could be so physically demanding. Dang, my feet throbbed.

My tiny refuge of space began to shrink as a group of cosplayers had the same idea and formed a small semi-circle near the bench. All five girls wore steampunk versions of different superheroes. Oh, whoa, custom mashup characters. Goggles, gears, and amazing leatherwork. How'd they make all that? In pictures, most costumes looked good, but those seemed straight out of a movie, like a professional had made them. But they were original characters—homemade.

One of the girls turned her back and whispered to the girl in a red, white, and blue leather corset. She snickered, and I made out the words "Off-the-rack."

"I'd buy a pre-made wig, but never a whole costume." The green-skinned girl whispered back.

A third steampunker spoke quieter than the other two. "…ya know…only the popular anime."

"Fake geek girl. I know the type."

The surroundings blurred into a haze, and I no longer sat in a convention among my peers. Behind me were the blue lockers in the middle school hallway from years ago. Groups of cosplayers became cliques, and conversations lowered into whispers and taunts. Any number of them could be glancing at me, laughing, or coming up with a new rumor. My stomach imploded, pulling my insides together in a tangled mess.

It wasn't middle school, though…right? These people were my friends. But, even if someone smiled in person, they could think something totally different. What if I ended up in a meme? Worst cosplay.

Miss pre-industrial America made a huge sigh, rolling her eyes. "The good photo-op spot was taken for an hour. They really should rope it off for the real cosplayers." She looked at me before turning her back.

Tears began to leak out, but I bit the inside of my cheek. Crying was worse. So much worse. But, I couldn't keep the dam shut, and water welled over my eyes. I covered my face with the gloves. *Stop, stop, stop.*

I pulled a hand away, thick black streaks down the fingers and palm of my glove. Shit. The makeup! Wiping my face, more foundation smudged with the black, and worse, the tears didn't stop. I was a total mess. If someone got a picture now, it'd be passed around before I could blink. I pulled my legs onto the bench and buried my face into my knees. My heart rate tripled, and shortened breaths caught into that damn repetitive loop where I could never get enough air in. No. Nonono. It hurt to breathe.

"Oh hey, isn't that one of the six-o-second guys?" One of the steampunk girls spoke louder.

"He's coming over here."

I heard rustling of fabric and jostling props from their group as they moved around. Closer? Further away? Oh please, don't let them come toward me. The tightness gripped my chest, wrapping pain around my ribs. I pictured the inevitable messages on my phone, links to posts about me. Rumors. Lies. Embarrassing truths.

If bad pictures made it online, it could follow me. Kids from my school could see them. My throat began to close from trying to keep the sob down.

A faint buzz preceded a tinny sounding voice from a speaker. "You're fixing to miss the cosplay panel if we don't hurry."

The schedule didn't show a cosplay panel for another hour, and that one was about making props. In the divot between the tops of my knees, I peered at the body standing a mere foot away. All I could make out was some distressed armor. Was he talking to me? Did he confuse me for someone else?

The speaker-voice echoed again. "Come on."

I pulled my hands away to see Boba Fett addressing *me*. His helmet, perfect movie-accurate armor, and even the voice—the whole costume was straight out of *Star Wars*. His hand reached out, and in a robotic motion, I took it. He pulled me to my feet and led me away from the bench, while the gaggle of mashup steampunk girls pointed and chattered among themselves. They sounded excited, not taunting like before.

Boba Fett kept hold of my hand through the crowd until we were all the way on the other side of the main thoroughfare, close to the escalators and the tunnel to the hotel. Once we stopped, I plucked my hand from his grip. He couldn't be Jake, since he and Cora didn't come to this con. Who was he anyway?

"T…thank." Huge, gloppy tears streamed down my cheeks. I wiped them again—smear city. It'd take heavy-duty bleach to clean it off the gloves. At least it didn't transfer anywhere else on the costume.

The echoey voice came out of Boba's speaker. "You okay?"

"Yes." I sniffed.

After an awkward pause came an electronic sigh. "Don't listen to them. I've seen 'em online, elitist jerks. That's not what cosplay's about. Cosplay's supposed to be for fun."

I nodded, my reflection doubling in the visor of his helmet. Around his neck hung a thick lanyard with his member badge; the name read "Aran." Nothing else, just one word. Definitely not Jake or anyone I knew.

He said, "For what it's worth, I think your costume is awesome."

"Thanks…"

The haze from before lingered longer than it should, and I couldn't shake that stupid feeling that everyone was talking about me. I glanced toward the artists' alley. People walked from one table to the next, some hurried down the hall to turn toward the gaming rooms, while a few seemed to mill about aimlessly. All were preoccupied with their own business. Why would they bother paying attention to me anyway? Last year, the school counselor had coached me to ignore those paranoid thoughts. I didn't need to go back to that, not when the con scene was usually the polar opposite of school.

A couple passed by, their costumes made of clothing from their closets or from a thrift store. Boba Fett was right. Cosplay was supposed to be fun. Supposed to be for everyone.

When I turned back, he'd disappeared. Where'd he go? He didn't have to pull me out of there, but he had. I could've relived the panic attacks from middle school. Instead, a simple compliment from a stranger reminded me why I did any of this to begin with. He asked for nothing and disappeared without a name except some badge handle that meant squat— Aran. I should've asked who he was, or thanked him…or said anything.

Cosplay for fun or not, I couldn't return to the floor with mascara smeared halfway down my cheeks, so I took a detour to the hotel room. The makeup remover towelettes possessed some kind of voodoo magic. In a few swipes, the black marks were gone. I splashed cold water onto my face, blinking the drops from my lashes. Cool. Refreshing. Only a little pink rimmed my eyes, which I could explain away with vigorous face washing or something. If Dan knew I had reverted to that mess of a girl, he'd get all protective again. I didn't need him trying to fight an enemy that didn't exist. It was my problem. I could get over it on my own.

Dan probably needed help at the booth by now. Besides, I didn't really feel like getting ready all over again, so I slipped on my *Infinity* T-shirt and headed for the dealers' room.

Tables butted against each other, forming squares of booths with aisles in-between. Shoppers stood on both sides of the walkway with other people loitering in the middle, and bodies, both costumed and in street duds, filled the room to capacity. I had to maneuver through the gauntlet of attendees and props to get to the rear of the ballroom.

Someone with a gigantic sword blocked the whole space in front of Uncle Rick's booth, so I army crawled under the front tablecloth. I slid two boxes out of my path and squirmed into the booth.

On the way to my feet, my head connected with Dan's leg.

He jumped a foot into the air. "You wanna give me a heart attack?"

I fixed my clothes. "Sorry. You can go do whatever. I'll man the booth." We were alone behind the table. "Where's Uncle Rick?"

"You changed out of costume?" Dan asked, "Why?"

In case my eyes did look weird, I faced the aisle instead of him. "Just got uncomfortable." I repeated, "Where's Uncle Rick?"

Dan cocked his head. "But you were so excited…"

"Drop it."

Silence cut between us like one of the axes for sale across the aisle. A girl browsed through the collectibles on the end of the table, and she picked out a pack of enamel pins. I rang her up.

"Great. Sign here." I held the clipboard for her scribble, and she left.

Dan straightened a few of the odds and ends that fell over, but didn't say anything for a minute. I shouldn't have snapped at him like that. What was wrong with me?

He kept his head down. "Dad went to pick up some burgers."

"Oh." I paused. "Okay."

Seemed like Dan planned to ignore my offer for him to go roam the con, but without his constant chatter, the weirdness between us grew unbearable. I wouldn't tell him what happened. He'd gotten me into cosplay in the first place, and he didn't need to think that something he did made me almost spiral down that hole again. After all, the panic attack let up before it got too bad.

What if Aran hadn't come then? My mind raced forward, pushing the what-if closer to reality, and I breathed shallow. My legs suddenly hurt. I'd been standing straight, knees locked.

Dan's worried frown returned, though he pretended not to notice.

I smiled and bent my knees, letting the slouch return to my posture. "Um, Dan?"

"What?"

"Do you know any Boba Fett cosplayers?" I asked.

Finally, a smile. "Depends on what you mean by 'know.' Online, yeah a ton, but none IRL."

"Oh."

"Was it an accurate costume?" Dan asked.

The image returned, burned into my mind. I'd never forget that face, well, helmet. I should have asked his name. "Yeah, like right out of the movie. The armor was molded plastic, very professional."

He went to the end of the booth and sorted through some fliers on the adjacent table. In the middle of a stack, he pulled out a black and red paper with Darth Vader's helmet and the Imperial insignia in the corner. "He's probably a member of the Six Hundred and Second Battalion. They've got a parade tomorrow morning."

Something lit inside me. I had to see him again, thank him. Maybe I could. "Really? Can you watch the booth?"

"Not a problem." Dan handed me the flyer. "So what's up with the Boba Fett guy?"

"He helped me out." I folded my fingers inside my hands to keep from grabbing at my shirt. "I just wanna thank him."

"Have fun then." Dan looked me over for a long minute and then shrugged. "Ya know, I think I am gonna check out that panel on *Doctor Who*. You'll be here?"

"Yeah."

Moving a touch too fast, he disappeared behind the curtain in the back. The fabric stopped swaying after a few seconds. An odd stillness replaced Dan's lively presence, and the space behind the booth seemed smaller than ever.

Kyle

The sun glinted off of a skyscraper and right into my visor, blinding me. Ghost-like blurs danced in my vision, and sweat dripped into my eyes. It burned. I shook my head and stumbled. The guy behind me grabbed my elbow so I didn't fall.

Clop, clop, clop.

Marching footsteps kept me grounded, and I followed the sound until my vision cleared. Even with my quarter-inch buzz cut, the helmet roasted my head like a piece of meat. Another drop of sweat formed on my forehead. The bugger decided to slide down my cheek and tickle my neck instead. How do the stormtroopers put up with the heat? The Mandalorian armor only covered my torso and left most of my arms and legs exposed to the cloth jumpsuit, which included strategically placed vents. Those guys had to be immune to chafing or something.

The parade route brought us all the way through the Dallas West End and then back to the hotel. The blasted humidity almost steamed me to death inside my costume, and the rest of the battalion must have felt the same. We all dragged our boots into the blessed air conditioning of the convention center. Some of the older guys took off parts of their costumes to cool down. Our garrison leader, Mike, looked especially sweaty with his peppered gray hair plastered to his head.

"Hey, Kyle." A clone trooper wearing a volunteer badge tapped my shoulder.

"Josh. What's up?" I grabbed my helmet but stopped. The crowd still surrounded us, most wanting pictures.

"I think someone's looking for you."

No one here knew me, except the other six-oh-second guys. "Who?" I scanned the crowd.

"There's a Sailor Moon asking about Aran."

"What?" The girl from yesterday was looking for me? Oh crap, I should've stayed around longer. But she had broken into tears; what's a guy supposed to do?

Josh added, "If I see her, I'll send her your way. Okay?"

"Sure." I looked toward the walls of the center. After getting cornered like that, she'd try to blend into the crowd. I would.

A few cameras flashed near me. I probably got in the shot, though I didn't bother to pose. Our battalion drew the photographers without any one of us having to put on a show. The lobby of the conference center stretched a hundred and fifty feet wide and longer the other direction. Normally, someone could maneuver easily though the large space, but the crowd created an ever-changing landscape of obstacles. Unpredictable. *Stupid subconscious.* There was nothing to be on guard about. I was at a convention surrounded by friends.

Through a few more bright flashes, a yellow head moved behind the barricade of people.

"Excuse me." I ducked past a few troopers, including Josh who lined up with his fellow clones for the photographers.

The yellow wig disappeared behind a couple of tall guys in the middle. I was right. I moved through the group, and there she stood. She seemed like she wanted to wait for the crowd to thin, but that wouldn't happen any time soon.

I walked toward her and halted, dragging the toe of my boot on the heavy-duty carpet. What was I thinking? Yesterday, those jerks harassed her, and then I fled the scene like a kid shoplifting candy from a mini-mart. She'd think I was an ass too. I turned around.

"Aran?" She'd spotted me.

No saving face now. "Yeah?" I pivoted, shoulders straight as a bounty hunter's, if bounty hunters had great posture. They did in the movie. Damn, I should say something first. What? Oh no, more silence.

"Thank you." The girl blurted it, like she'd held her breath and finally exploded.

Thank you? *Thank me?* I only did what anyone with half a brain would've. No one deserves to feel alone like that. No one.

"Uh. Um." *Very eloquent.* I inhaled. "Are you okay?"

She nodded. "I had to find you to say thanks. I froze yesterday, and if you hadn't shown up…" She held onto her arm, black stains visible on the glove's fingertips.

"I'm sorry I left you. I, uh. Sorry…didn't know what else to say." More eloquence. I unhooked and re-snapped the holster for my prop blaster, again. It kept me from finding something weirder to do with my hands.

"It's okay. I was embarrassed anyway." The girl smiled, but not that fake anime one the other cosplayers use. The openness in her oval face brought the character to life. Instead of some representation of a cartoon, she pulled the drawing into reality and fleshed out a two-dimensional thing into a real person.

Wait…she wore the Sailor Moon costume again? "I'm glad you didn't let those elitist jerks ruin cosplaying for you."

She pulled the edges of her skirt. "I thought you wouldn't recognize me without it."

"Will you give it up, now that you thanked me?"

Instead of an answer, she grabbed hold of her arm. The closed-off body language shouted loud and clear.

"Don't," I said, the microphone sending feedback in my ear. "We all have our reasons for wanting to take on a character, and no matter what they are, don't stop because'a some girls who want to ruin things for everyone."

"I really like cosplaying, bu—"

"Then keep on." The speaker made my voice sound hollow, even to me. I took the helmet off, and sweet air from heaven kissed my face.

She blinked. Maybe she thought I was older, which made sense. Wearing body armor and a helmet pretty much gave away my height, leaving the rest of my demographics a mystery. I showed her my badge. "See this? Aran is Mando'a for 'Guard.' It's perfect."

"What's perfect?"

"I'll be your bodyguard, and you can walk the convention without any worries."

Sailor Moon let go of her arm and stretched a little taller. "Thank you…Aran."

"Kyle." I cradled the helmet in my left arm and reached to shake with my right.

She took my hand. "Audrey."

Over the next few hours, we roamed the main floor of the convention. Perhaps roam was a generous term. We'd walk a few yards in one direction and then have to stop for pictures. As soon as someone asked for a photo, Audrey changed from a shy girl into an actress, full of exaggerated movement and a cute laugh to match. Her joy radiated outward as a contagious energy. I got into it too, posing, saying lines from the movie. Usually I'd just stand with the guys for a few pics. I guess I hadn't been a true "cosplayer," if there was such a thing.

During a lull between flashes, a little girl somewhere in the preschool range took careful steps toward us like we were aliens and she had a chance at first contact.

Her mother waved her forward. "Don't be nervous, sweetheart. Ask her."

The girl hugged a puffy notebook to her body. "Sailor Moon? Um, can you…" she held the book and matching feathery pen toward Audrey.

"What's this?" Audrey asked.

"Sign. Please."

Audrey covered her mouth and glanced at me as her surprise shifted into a grin. Opening the book, she turned to the girl. "What's your name?"

"Rae."

She signed in huge loopy letters "Sailor Moon," dotting the *i* with a heart, and took a picture with the girl. Little Rae hopped away with her mom, and the whole lobby could hear her excited squeaks as she replayed her encounter with the real, live Sailor Moon.

After another series of photos, Audrey went to freshen up in the bathroom. Gamers gathered around tables at the far end of the hall, some playing collectible card games and others taking up three tables with full Warhammer sets. Miniatures battled one another atop textbook mountains and Styrofoam cups standing in for various terrains. An entire world existed for the tiny combatants, their owners tossing dice to determine the fate of their battle. The orc army clearly had the advantage with the high ground.

Along the other wall, volunteers strung rope between metal stands to make a queue for the media panel slated for later that night. Eager fans couldn't wait to get in line.

To the side, a cosplayer in a complex X-Men costume had the attention of a large number of people. It looked kinda like armor, with big-ass shoulder pauldrons. And he wore movie-quality silver makeup. He posed, like Audrey had, but fell flat. No energy, no life. Why was he so different?

Audrey's voice came from my side. "Ready?"

I startled. "Sure. Where to now?"

"I've gotta work this afternoon, but I thought I could catch trivia in room G."

"Work?"

She held up her badge, which plainly read "Dealer" on the bottom. It even had a different picture on the front, a character waving a flag instead of the battle-ready warrior on mine. *Look who wins the Most Observant trophy.*

A snort escaped. "I didn't notice the badge, and I'm supposed to be your bodyguard. Glad I work for free now, aren't ya?"

"You get what you pay for." She shrugged with no hint of a smile.

I stuttered, and she laughed. There it was, a growing smirk that came out of hiding.

"Maybe I'll charge you after all. Incompetence like this ain't cheap, ya know." I chuckled. "Come on, let's go play trivia." I reached to take her hand.

Her arm tensed at my touch. I did too. Did she want me to do that? She kept hold of my hand, though it was a light grip, but didn't pull away.

We were both wearing gloves, so maybe that made it not a big deal. It wasn't a big deal. But then, why was my heart pounding? Why was I second guessing?

Kyle, get a grip!

I guided her through a group of people toward the meeting rooms. Audrey squeezed my hand, small fingers pulled tight against my palm. Warm, even through the layers. We arrived in room G, a breakout space like all the others. The room contained about fifty chairs in hotel floral upholstery, and two people sat near one of the fold-out walls by the front stage. A moderator waited with a microphone and a stack of index cards. Behind him, a white board leaned on a rickety easel. He asked for our names and wrote them on the board with the others. Audrey's name appeared next to mine, separated by a thin black line.

He checked his watch and picked up the mic. "Looks like a small group today, but that means a bigger challenge for you guys." He raised his voice. "Y'all ready for trivia?"

The four of us bobbed our heads in varying nods. Crickets chirped.

"I said, are y'all *ready!*"

"Yeah!" Audrey matched his volume. The other two echoed quiet responses. I never pegged Audrey to be the first to break the ice, especially around a group. She seemed so shy.

"With four participants, we don't have to drag out the bells. I can see who raises a hand first. Let's get started." The moderator shuffled the index cards and pulled one off the top. "In the SyFy channel show *Defiance*, how many Voltan races occupy Earth?"

One of the guys by the stage raised his hand. The moderator pointed for him to answer. "Six."

The mod struck tick in his column. "One point. Next question, in the X-Men comics, what do they call the original, or main, universe?"

Audrey's hand shot up a second before the other guys. "Six-Sixteen."

"Right." A tick marked under her name.

So, she's into comics. Cool.

"I got a *Star Wars* question here. Bet Boba Fett's gonna know this one," the moderator chuckled. "What planet is Han Solo from?"

I raised my hand, but the moderator pointed slightly to my left.

Audrey chirped, "Corellia."

"Right again. You're on a roll. Too slow on the draw, Boba." The mod added another tick under her name. *Star Wars* too?

The rest of the trivia contest continued to surprise me. Though the other contestants got a few questions, Audrey blew the rest of us away. She knew answers from sci-fi, comics, anime, and some obscure series I'd never heard of. She only missed a few fantasy questions, most from the Hobbit movies. When I first saw her dressed in an anime costume, an old one too,

I guessed that was her thing, an otaku all the way. So very wrong. *Everything* was her "thing."

At the end, the moderator shook Audrey's hand and gave her a framed certificate naming her trivia champion of the convention. She trotted back to the doorway, where I waited for her.

We walked down the hall, neither leading the way and with no particular direction to go. If she didn't need to go anywhere, I wasn't gonna rush it. "Is there anything at these conventions you don't know about?" I asked to ask something, so the awkward pauses wouldn't break the flow.

She pursed her lips, stopped, and said, "Hentai."

I cough-laughed, choking on stray spit. "Ha ha. Of course. Yeah…" I shook my head. "Me neither. I don't even know what that is."

Audrey let the silence hang a moment. "If you didn't know what anime porn was, why'd you freak out?" That little smirk from before crept into the corner of her lip.

"Oh yeah, your *'I know nothing'* act is losing steam now."

"Knowing and watching are different things, Jon Snow." She stopped for a second to let a group squeeze past us into the hall. We arrived out in the main lobby. "Quick lunch? I don't have to be back in the booth 'til one."

I took her free hand without pause. "There's a yaki-ramen stand outside the dealers' room."

"I love that stuff."

Of course she did. Next thing I knew, we walked hand-in-hand and side-by-side through convention lobby. Whatever fear she felt before had evaporated like sweat from the morning parade, gone into the air. Under my helmet, my cheeks began to hurt. How long had I been smiling like that?

Some other attendees found places to eat at the tables unoccupied by RPG books, miniatures, or card games. We took our plastic boxes of fried ramen and found an open seat at the end of one of their tables.

"It's gonna be hard to eat with that helmet on." Audrey snapped open her wooden chopsticks, scraping the ends to remove splinters.

"Ha. Ha. I was fixing to." I yanked it off and set it to the side next to her certificate. "Congratulations. That was quite impressive."

With her chopsticks holding a wad of ramen in her mouth, she raised a brow. She gulped down her bite. "Impressive? Not the usual comment I'd hear at school for that kind of thing."

"I'm wearing Mandalorian armor. I have a different opinion of 'cool' than the popular kids." The edges of my lips hurt. Was I still smiling like an idiot? I filled my mouth with a bite of ramen. Sweet and sour teriyaki, so good.

Audrey chuckled. "True, true. My uncle owns a comic store, well, not really my 'uncle,' but I call him that. The family friend kind. Anyway, he gave me a job. I was into anime and stuff way before then, but now I have unlimited access."

"Oh." I pointed my chopstick at her. "Unfair advantage. That's why I lost."

"You lost because you had three points."

"Three honestly-earned points, I might add."

She waved her hand in the air. "I surrender. The certificate is yours." The hidden smile in her pink lips said otherwise.

"Kidding aside, you were awesome."

Audrey looked startled and then made an extra effort to brush her wig pigtails over her shoulders. "Thanks."

Muffled music came from under the table, and my belt pouch buzzed. I unclipped the pocket to retrieve the phone, playing "The Imperial March"—Darth Vader's theme. Crap. Did Dad figure out I went to the con anyway? Aunt Beth was gonna cover for me.

I hit *Ignore*.

"What generation iPhone is it?" Audrey asked.

"Five. I hope they improved Siri in later versions." I set the phone on the table and picked up my chopsticks.

"They did." She paused. "Can I see it?"

"Sure."

She looked through the phone, swiping her finger past the different icons. A girl was holding my phone, a cute girl who had the same interests. Damn, it sounded so analytical like that. The bites of ramen I'd taken began to squirm.

"So, uh." Aha, the beauty of speech once again within my power. "While you've got it, um…you could enter your number." I added, "If you want."

Audrey focused on the screen, hard, and tapped in her information. When she finished, she slid it across the table.

"It's almost time for my shift. I've gotta go." She stood. Her plastic container had a third of the ramen left uneaten.

"Right. Okay."

Her big red bow raised and lowered with a breath. "I have to help pack up the booth, but I'm free tomorrow in the morning. Would you want to explore the con with me?"

Instead of yelling 'yes, yes, yes,' I vibrated my head in a weird nod. "Sure."

She returned a similar up-down head shake. "I'll be by the fountain in the lobby at eight-thirty."

"See ya tomorrow." The words floated out of my mouth, and in another disembodied moment, she was gone. *What just happened? Did I make a date? Wait, she asked me…who cares.* Nervous energy coursed through my body, and I was probably shaking enough for everyone to notice. But no, only I could feel the electricity.

Tomorrow, tomorrow I had a date.

Under my hand, the imperial march started up again. Dad. The nerves amped up in to full-blown worry. I inhaled and exhaled slowly. No matter what Dad's problem was this time, he could handle it.

I hit *Ignore*.

Kyle

The clock on my phone read just about eight-thirty. I'd been dressed and ready for an hour, and after tightening the belt one last time, I put on my helmet and headed to the lobby. The sun sparkled through the skylight, casting rays across the sparse tile floor. A lone con-goer strolled by the elevator bank and blocked my view of the fountain.

Then I saw her. A girl without the yellow pigtails perched on the rounded stone edge surrounding the tinkling fountain. Her straight hair brushed past her shoulders, and the natural light varied the browns, like the bark of a tree with deep grooves and pale ridges. Instead of that bright costume, she wore a black T-shirt and jeans. She stood out anyway.

My boots clicked as I walked closer.

Audrey turned her head, and her cheeks perked up with a smile. Not the smile she gave the cameras, though that one emitted energy to rival the flashes. Now, her face filled with something vibrant, something warm. Did she blush?

Inside the helmet, my ears burned. I glanced toward the check-in desk, so maybe it wouldn't be painfully obvious I'd been watching her. Maybe she'd still think I was cool. That was, *if* she thought that.

"Hey." Audrey stood and brushed the dust from her jeans with one hand, the other occupied with a cup of Starbucks. Her free hand tapped the side of her leg.

"Mornin'."

She gestured to the café counter with her disposable cup. "I know it's early. Want one? My treat."

"Great idea. Thanks." My voice sounded sharp and robotic. How could she gauge my tone through the speaker? I followed after her and took off the helmet, shoving it under the crook of my left arm.

On the counter, stacks of cups formed a display next to four insulated thermoses of different coffee blends. The stacks varied in height, like a bar chart illustrating drink-size popularity. From the shortest one, I grabbed a medium, or *grande* due to obsessive corporate marketing, and filled it with Italian roast, darkest of the dark.

"Oh, you can get a latte or something from the shop instead of the cheap stuff. I've got a caramel brulée. They sprinkle toasted sugar on top, and it melts in your mouth." Audrey took a sip of her frou-frou drink. A drop of foam stuck to her sparkling lip. She didn't wear the thick makeup from yesterday, only whatever shiny stuff she put on her lips. Lip glitz? No, that didn't sound right.

"Kyle?"

"Oh, yeah no. This is the good stuff." I snapped a lid on the cup and slipped on a cardboard sleeve.

Audrey paid at the cash register. If this was a date, I already screwed up. I'd pay for lunch. Yeah, that'd fix it.

Together we strolled out of the lobby and down the corridor to the convention center. The dealers' room had opened only a few minutes before, so most of the early birds went straight for the double doors. The usually crowded hall felt still as a pond, where the slight movement of artists behind their tables sent ripples curling across the surface in expanding concentric circles. Every sound amplified without the waves of attendees. Whispers became shouts, footsteps echoed, and the air conditioner rumbled in the vents above, like thunder in a cloudless sky. Eerie, but peaceful too.

We ambled to the art displays. I wanted to hold Audrey's hand, but my right held the coffee and my left the helmet. I should've left it in the room.

Audrey didn't seem to notice. She perused the prints on the table. "Oh, look. It's the Avengers but with Sailor Senshi costumes. I'd do the Iron Man one in a heartbeat."

"How 'bout Hulk. Then you could go all out with green face paint."

"Thought you'd want that one." She pointed to the green-skinned drawing in the little purple skirt. "The color would look great in your buzz-cut."

I almost spat out my coffee. "I ain't wearing a sailor scout costume."

She giggled. "Just kidding. You'd have to be Tuxedo Mask." She flipped through the folder of prints, which started showing different pastel ponies dressed as *Star Trek* captains. "What cosplay would you want to do next?"

"Me?" I adjusted the grip on my helmet. "I've only done Boba. I like doing six-oh stuff."

Behind us, someone shouted. A guy dashed out of the breakout-room hallway, hugging a backpack. Someone in a uniform chased after him—a security guard?

The guy with the backpack ran in our direction, dodging errant chairs. He moved too close to the tables.

Audrey turned and stepped to the side, right in his way. "What's—"

His trajectory…he was gonna crash into us. I put my arm up to block her, but the guy slammed into my back as he ran by, knocking us to the ground between two artists' tables. Someone tripped over my outstretched legs as voices shouted from further down the hall, probably where the guy kept running.

"Argh!" The security guard yanked his ankle free from mine.

"Ow." Audrey grabbed her shoulder.

I scrambled up and helped her to her feet. "You okay?"

She nodded.

The guard cursed again. "Did you see which way he went?"

None of the artists spoke up, because they were probably too busy watching us fall. I'd heard the commotion from one direction, but that could've been something else. I didn't know for sure, and misguiding him would be bad.

I shook my head, too.

"Thanks anyway." The guard hurried off down one of the hallways to search for the thief. Whatever he stole, it must be a big deal.

"That's more excitement than I've ever had at a con," Audrey said.

"Me too." I withdrew my gaze from the guard back to her.

Audrey pinched at her shirt. She tugged it from her body where wet fabric clung to her skin. Her hair stuck to her neck and the sides of her face. The coffee! Both of our cups rolled empty on the floor.

"Did it burn you?" I reached toward her but stopped.

"No. It wasn't hot anymore." She squeezed the edge of the shirt. Brown liquid dripped onto the floor, and she kept chewing her lip.

Why didn't I get her further away? I could have said "move" or pushed her out of the way or even tried to stop the thief myself. I picked up the helmet to hold something. My fingers fidgeted with the seam on the side, unable to get the damn hint and keep still.

She sighed. "I don't have another shirt to wear. I only brought this one and my costume."

"I got a free shirt for pre-registering. It's still rolled up from the registration bag. You can have it." I rattled on. "It'll be huge though, extra large."

"Really?" Audrey's mouth parted.

"Yeah, of course. It's in my room just past the lobby, ground floor."

She smiled.

My heart skipped.

Once in the hallway, my pulse quickened. I asked a girl to my hotel room? Oh no, that's not what I meant. What if she thought? Oh crap. She might think I was a creep. She wouldn't think that, right? We hadn't known each other long, so maybe she would. I tapped the blaster's holster and swallowed a few more times than necessary.

At the door, I reached in my belt pouch for the key card and accidentally dropped it on the floor. The armor made it hard to bend, so I needed to kneel to pick it up. She had to be staring at me.

"It won't take long for me to find it. You can wait out here, or come in." There, now she wouldn't be confused. *Please don't think I'm some skeezy weirdo.*

She nodded. "Sure."

I opened the door, and she grabbed the edge as I went it, holding it open for herself. Guess she chose to come, too.

"Let me get it real fast." I ran to the dresser on the far wall and carefully lifted a stack of folded shirts. It wouldn't be packed with my pants in the other drawer either. Where did I put it up? She was waiting there behind me, soaked, and probably watching me search like I had no clue where the shirt went. Which was true, no idea. Maybe I put it up in the tote bag.

Taking care not to slam the mirrored closet, I slid it open. The tote leaned against the side, and I scoured through it until my hands landed on the rolled-up shirt bound with rubber bands. Victory!

I turned around, prize in hand. Standing with her back to the door, Audrey was wringing the ends of her shirt, and coffee dripped onto the floor. Tan stains with hints of foam left lines down the sides of her face and neck.

"It even got in your hair. I'm so sorry." I dropped the shirt and lunged across the tiny entryway into the bathroom to grab a towel off the rack. I wiped the brown streaks off her neck. "This is all my fault."

"It's okay."

Soft fingers touched the back of my hand. I slid the towel across her cheek with gentle pressure as she watched me with wide chestnut eyes. She didn't say anything. Neither did I. My hand gripped tighter on the towel, but I had stopped cleaning. Everything stopped.

Audrey's glitzed lips opened, like she meant to say more. So pretty. Should I kiss her? I leaned in, only an inch.

"Right." She shook her head as if snapping out of a daze. "Thank you."

My heart resumed beating, and I jumped back a foot. "Yeah. No problem." I knelt to grab the shirt from the floor and, in stop-motion stills, handed it over.

"Can I change in the bathroom real quick?" Audrey held the bundled shirt in front of her, between us.

I must have read the whole thing wrong. What was I thinking? Heat flooded my face. "Yeah, sure."

She slipped inside and the door clicked locked.

Maybe now my heart would slow. The image popped into my head of her looking into my eyes…pink beautiful lips. I put my hand over my chest and felt it through the plastic armor. No, my heart would never slow again.

Audrey

Once inside the bathroom, I peeled off my wet shirt and dropped it onto the floor with a *sloopsh*. Crap, the coffee had soaked the side of my bra a nice tan color. Couldn't do anything about that now, so I slipped Kyle's giant white shirt over my head. Then I caught a look at the mirror. Oh no. I ran my fingers through the rat's nest that used to be hair.

Is that how he saw me a second ago, disheveled with clumps of hair matted to my head? He stared at me for a zillion years. It must have been my hair.

He'd leaned in though, like they do in movies before a—*Wake up Audrey!* So I liked him, but that in no way meant he felt the same. We just met, and I asked *him* out. Kinda, sorta, out…at the con. My reflection turned a shade of pink that would've matched the Power Ranger costume.

I turned on the tap and splashed cold water on my face, using my trusted "start fresh" technique. I blotted my face with a towel. There, the blush vanished.

Breathing deep, I opened the door, my wet shirt balled between my hands. Kyle finished folding a pair of jeans into a pile on the bed. He smiled, his tennis-ball head tilted to one side. Part of me wanted to rub the buzz cut and feel his fuzzy hair under my fingers, but the less-crazy part held me back. Even Sailor Moon wasn't brave enough to do that.

Kyle grabbed his helmet from the dresser, and after looking at me, he winced. "I didn't see the shirt before. Sorry the con mascot is a half-dressed elf chick."

"As long as I'm dressed." I fixed the bottom of the shirt over my butt. "Thanks again."

"Glad I could help." He opened the door, and we left the room behind.

In the hallway, I filled in the space beside him, letting us walk together without either asking. On auto, we strolled through the lobby and into the convention space, which now hummed with activity, and the horde of people made it seem as though that empty version never existed. The whole chase thing happened in a dream or one of the animes showing in the video rooms. Even the con funk had returned with a vengeance.

"The con really packed up fast, didn't it?" I said.

Kyle nodded as he stared into the distance. "Yeah, like it never happened."

"I was thinking the same thing." I pointed to the booth where the guy almost ran me down. Someone in a Godzilla costume with his girlfriend dressed as Mothra perused the artists' tables. "You wouldn't have room to tackle me now."

Kyle went stiff, like I gave him a heart attack. "I didn't, that guy ran into…"

"I'm just kidding. You did block me with those fast reflexes. Something you learned in the six-oh-second?"

He closed his mouth, his eyes glancing down and to the side. He blinked and his smile returned as if that sideways frown had never crossed his face. "Oh no, the group is a formal cosplayer organization. There's no training or anything like that."

I followed him to the dealers' room but stopped short of going in. "Ah cool. Um, I'll have enough of that when I'm packing up. Wanna do something else?"

"Sure. What?"

"I forgot to eat breakfast. Wanna get some snacks and huddle down on the floor out of the way?" I didn't tell him half that excitement was waiting for him in the morning. Good thing I didn't eat earlier. My stomach had folded in on itself like origami from overthinking things. Did I overthink it? What was *he* thinking? Maybe I was just a pity case.

He seemed relaxed, plopping quarters into the slot to buy some Cheetos. What did I expect, for a neon sign to appear over his head? He looked as unreadable as any other guy in the world. Why was I so bad at this?

All the tables used for gaming yesterday had been cleared away. By the hallway to the breakout rooms, two ugly upholstered chairs butted against a fake tree in a wicker basket. A girl in a Nyan Cat hoodie sat cross legged in one, knitting something out of fuzzy purple yarn, and her friend lounged in the other, draping her legs over the armrest. However, the floor beside the chairs was open and out of the flow of traffic.

We grabbed our snacks and claimed a spot a few feet from the chairs. I pinched the foil wrapper at the seam to open my Cheez-its and ate a couple. Salt coated my lips, and the cheddar taste bit sour into my cheek, the flavor of mild rebellion. Mom never let me get junk at home.

Opposite me, Kyle piled his snacks between his legs. He'd gotten Cheetos, a bag of cream cookies, and a king-size Reese's Cup pack. He dug into the cheesy goodness first, just like I had. I tried not to stare. Would we sit in silence until we finished eating? What should I say? Maybe I could talk about the closing ceremonies.

"Can I ask you something?" Kyle blurted. "I mean, as long as you won't think I'm weird for asking."

I met his gaze, and he glanced away. "With a preamble like that, you have to."

He ran his palm over his fuzz-ball head. "Is this…a date?"

Holy cow, did he just out and say it? Using the heel of my hand, I wiped the salt from my lips and blocked my twitchy jaw. "If that's okay with you?"

"Yeah. Yeah." A huge grin exploded on his face, and he laughed. "Never been more nervous in my life."

"Me neither." I chuckled, too. What a pair of scaredy-cats we made. A pair. A couple. Warm tingles ran through my veins all the way to my fingertips.

Kyle scooted closer, being careful to keep his snacks balanced in his lap. A loud *ping* came from the phone in his belt pouch, and being so close, I felt its vibration on my side. He crunched another Cheeto, smiling at me with orange powder on his lips and some on his nose.

A little wrinkle popped between his brows. "What is it? Is there something on my face?"

I tapped my nose.

He wiped and saw the orange on his palm. "This stuff gets everywhere, I swear."

"Coffee and cheese snacks, what food groups have we covered today?" I took another bite, relishing the taste.

Clearing his throat, he concentrated on his pile of snacks. "Guess I'll have to take you somewhere for a real meal next time."

Little bubbles popped in my stomach, until I found my voice. "Yeah. I'd love that." He wanted to take me on a real date?

Kyle's phone pinged and vibrated again. And again. And again.

After wiping his hand on the carpet, he leaned sideways to grab his phone from the pouch. As he read the messages, the glow of the screen reflected a stark change. The goofy smile was gone, and the orange streaks looked weird on his new expression…worried, frightened, or sick. Something not good.

"Everything okay?" I asked.

Kyle jumped to his feet, and the snacks rained to the floor, crumbs sprinkling everywhere. "I gotta go. Sorry."

"What's—"

"I'm so sorry. I'll text." He shoved his phone in his pouch and ran down the hall, swallowed by a wall of people.

What the heck just happened? What could that message have said that'd make him leave like that? Was he in trouble? Did someone get hurt?

An uncomfortable itch crawled over my skin. He'd probably tell me later, since he said he'd text. I reached over to pick up the snacks and saw his Boba Fett helmet. Oh no, he'd left it behind, and I didn't get his number. He probably didn't get too far, and he had to be going to the parking garage. If I hurried, I'd catch him.

I hugged the helmet and jogged through the convention center toward the tunnel out. The distance seemed to grow the further I ran, and everyone stood in the worst possible places, like they meant to be in my way. I stopped saying excuse me, pushing past the last few people with my elbow, and broke into the open area by the parking garage elevators. No time to wait. I hefted open the heavy door to the stairwell and hurried down.

As I shoved through the door to the garage, an idling engine rumbled, and a deep voice said, "Get in."

A black pickup the size of a house straddled the center lane of the garage, roaring loud in the closed space. Kyle was standing by the opened passenger door. I couldn't see the driver.

Kyle wrapped his arms around his stomach, and he looked like he was going to vomit.

"Now," the driver ordered.

When Kyle didn't make a move, the bald man in the truck reached over and grabbed Kyle's arm, pulling him inside. The door slammed closed.

"Wait!" I ran to the curb, and the truck peeled away in a cloud of exhaust. I coughed, eyes stinging. They were gone.

Holy crap. Though Kyle looked like he knew the guy, he didn't go willingly. Was this happening? Like, in real life? Did I just see that?

My heart raced at the same speed as the thoughts firing one after another. It was probably his dad or grandfather or someone picking him up. Totally normal. But, Kyle got those messages and seemed afraid, no…terrified. Was someone hurt, sick, dying? Something horrible might've happened, and I couldn't even text to make sure he was okay.

Hugging his helmet to my chest, I wandered back up the stairwell to the lobby, the scene replaying. Though I only saw the back of Kyle's head, he had closed in on himself. The man told him to get in the truck. I didn't hear, but maybe he said "no." Did he shake his head? The driver had to grab Kyle to get him inside. Oh no, no. Did he get kidnapped?

Rational and irrational scenarios twisted together, and my throat closed into a slide-whistle. Is there some kind of custody battle thing, maybe like with those ten-year-old twins on the news? The mother went nuts and left the country with the kids. That could've happened. Either way, Kyle might need help.

I hurried to the convention center, but ten-zillion people formed an impenetrable blob. I had to get through. My heart beat so fast I couldn't breathe. I couldn't shout for anyone to move. My head felt muffled and cloudy, drowning in a sea of people. Someone pushed from behind, knocking me into three people, though we all miraculously stayed on our feet, the helmet fell to the floor. I bent to grab it, but it got kicked away. I got on my hands and knees and crawled through a pair of legs, snatching the helmet away from getting crushed. There, an opening in the crowd. I took a breath and forged onward.

Chaos greeted me inside the dealers' room. The last-minute deals packed the ballroom full, even more than the area outside. I fought through a swarm of sweaty fanboys to get behind the table and squirmed between two guys to duck under the table skirt. Before I got to my feet, Dan and Uncle Rick almost stepped on me, twice. Each.

"Someone took him!" I was still shaking.

"Took who?" Dan handed a bag to a customer.

"Kyle, he—"

Uncle Rick thrust a clipboard into my hand, and the pen fell into the mess at my feet. "You're late. Just help us ring these people up. We've got a line and can maybe make it into the black."

I huffed. "It's important."

Uncle Rick ignored me again to keep messing with that damn credit card machine. Kyle could be in trouble. Didn't he care?

"You have to listen!" I threw the clipboard to the ground, or more accurately, right into Dan's foot.

"Ow!" Dan bent, hitting me with his elbow.

I stumbled on another stupid box. My butt hit the floor, and I knocked the rack behind me into the black curtain.

Pop! Pop! Snap!

In slow motion, the backdrop swirled down over us, like the swathes of fabric the acrobats dance upon in Cirque du Solei. Then darkness, a moment of silence, and—wait for it—

laughter. A few voices cried, "are you okay," but the majority laughed, hard too, not the polite chuckle you try to hide when a waiter drops a tray.

I flailed my arms, trying to free myself from the heavy curtain, but I couldn't find my way out. It twisted around my legs and got caught between the crud piled inside the booth. My lungs constricted each breath shorter. What had I done?

Oh shit, I just destroyed the booth.

The weight lifted, and fabric slid over my head, hair brushing into my face. Through the tangled mess, I saw Uncle Rick pulling at the backdrop. He slammed the gigantic wad on top of an uneven stack of crates, which teetered but didn't collapse. Half the merchandise on the table had fallen off, and the rest scattered both inside and outside the booth.

Dan grabbed my elbow to steady me.

Uncle Rick put on a smile for the customers, but he shook beneath the surface. He only picked at his graying beard when he wanted to keep from exploding, and he was trying to pick that thing clean off.

"Not very neat, but the sales are still on. I can find what you wanted if you give me a second." Uncle Rick grabbed one of the toppled bobble heads from a pile on the floor.

I knelt to right a plastic tub that used to be full of buttons. "I'm sorry."

"Don't." Uncle Rick snatched the bin from my hands. "You and Dan just go."

His shaking had stopped, but I'd prefer his anger to the look he had now. Deep wrinkles sliced across his forehead, and a skin of water pooled over his eyes.

"I'm so sorry. I'll help clean." I stood up, trying hard not to crush anything.

Next to me, Dan said, "I bumped her. It was my fault."

"There's no room for all of us in this, so just go." Uncle Rick knelt into the mess, turning toward the customer with a fake smile. "Did you want anything else?"

While I had conquered the anxiety response, instead an uncomfortable I-failed-a-test feeling churned my stomach into an acid factory. "But—"

"Go."

Dan gently grasped my upper arm. He shook his head. We really had to leave.

Kyle's helmet was lost somewhere under the mountain of merchandise, but I'd have to get it later. Following Dan, I exited into an adjacent booth. We nodded apologies to the owners, found a crack between a pair of tables, and went into the aisle.

With his hand still firm on my arm, Dan guided me into the service hall the vendors use to bring in merchandise from their trucks. It wasn't time to break down yet, so the door to the loading dock was closed. The thin wall muffled the commotion from the ballroom.

Dan released my arm. "Dad's over stressed, don't feel bad. It wasn't your fault."

"No, it was." That look Uncle Rick gave said I'd ruined everything, which again turned my stomach into acid town. But, that wasn't the important thing right now. The image popped into my head—the bald man dragging Kyle into the truck. I started shaking again.

"Audrey?"

"Kyle!" I rushed forward, accidentally backing Dan into the wall. "Out in the garage, somebody made him get in a truck. He knew the man, but Kyle looked scared out of his mind. What if he was kidnapped? What if they make him leave the country?"

"Wait, slow down. Who's Kyle?"

"My…" *Was he my boyfriend? Yes? No?* I shook my head. "The Boba Fett guy. He could be in trouble. Should we call the police?" Jitters ran through me from my fingers to my toes and even my face.

Dan held up his palms, so I'd back up. "Whoa, whoa, hold it. You said he knew the guy in the truck, right?"

"Yeah."

"It was probably his father or a guardian picking him up. I know you're 'worst case scenario' girl, but let's not jump to conclusions, okay? Remember what the counselor said."

I nodded, though I didn't feel any better. "Okay."

Dan smoothed his hand over his wild curls. "Do you know his number?"

"No." And I had his Boba Fett helmet to give him.

After a long pause, Dan nodded. "Okay. I'll contact my cosplayer friends and see if anyone knows him."

A lightness blossomed inside, and I leapt forward to hug him. "Thank you!"

He patted me on the back and gently pulled away. "Let's go out to the con 'til Dad needs us." His voice seemed less energetic than usual. Of course, Uncle Rick had yelled at him, too.

"Thank you so much."

"No problem, really." He turned to walk toward the exit leading to the convention, and I followed only a foot behind. In the empty hall, the space between us seemed much wider.

7

Kyle

The bedroom door clicked closed behind me, giving way to normal quiet. The silence in the truck cab all the way home to Waco had dropped below the existence of sound into the vacuum of space. I'd apologized, again and again, just to be met with pained glances and tightened lips.

I drug my feet to the twin-sized bed and flopped onto the *Star Wars* comforter I'd had since I was six. The blue of space had faded into a daylight sky speckled with graying stars, and a big stain blotted half of the Death Star. I'd never get rid of it even if the old thing disintegrated into threads.

Above me, the popcorn ceiling's thousands of little bumps looked like alien terrain in a faraway galaxy. When I was younger, I'd imagine walking on that planet, leaving footprints in the gravel or finding alien life hiding in the shadows. Escapism can only take a kid so far though, and eventually I grew up.

But maybe now I didn't have to pretend alone. I could talk to someone else, vent or at least escape into her life by listening to her stories. Audrey. I reached into my pocket. Right, Dad took my phone, which I deserved for lying, but he abandoned my car at the hotel, too. Before the silent treatment, he'd said I needed to learn humility. Suppose begging for rides home would do it.

But what about Audrey? I finally found someone I liked, who liked me, and it ended before it began. No phone, no phone number, and she didn't give me any other way to contact her. I hadn't asked. Idiot. I should've given her mine, although calling my cell wouldn't do her much good now.

The laptop sat lifeless across the room. I could open it up, play a game, screw around on the internet, or maybe finish the English paper due next week. But my body wouldn't move. I couldn't will it to. After a while, the guilt eating me up seemed to numb, and my alien world blurred to nothing.

A knock woke me.

"Kyle. Dinner!" Dad called from outside the door.

I rolled onto my stomach. The smell of sweaty pillow pressed into my nose. My face felt hot, and I likely had weird creases in my cheek from the fabric. I sat up, yawning, and the Death Star caught my eye. Didn't want Dad to see it, so I pulled the sheet over to cover the comforter and walked to the door.

"What's for dinner?" I asked, opening the door.

Dad's six-foot frame filled the hallway. His frown had eased up, and he seemed normal again. "Got some of those frozen steaks all grilled up. Oh, and peanut butter cup ice cream for dessert."

"Sounds good." Maybe he'd forgive me? I hadn't meant to mess things up for his election. Why would cosplay have any effect on the city council run anyway? But whatever.

"The Cowboys are on, too. We can make a night of it." Rubbing a palm on his bald head, he smiled. Was that one real? He could flip from okay to depressed in a millisecond…it was hard to keep up.

Gotta fake it 'til ya make it, so I smiled too. "Okay, sure."

Football, of course. I'd put up with the boring hours of men in tights slamming into one another for his benefit. He must know I didn't care, but pretending made him happy. I could at least do that.

We slid the steaks off the electric grill onto our plates and took our appropriate seats in the living room, me on the sofa, him in the recliner next to a tray table. Dad cracked open a beer before the first down, and he handed me a root beer so I could join in with the tradition without breaking the law. It'd probably look bad if the city council board member, the lawyer's kid, drank alcohol.

"Come on! Can't y'all catch the damn ball!" he yelled.

"Yeah," I added to the chorus.

Dad took a sip and smiled at me. Looked like I managed to help him get in a good mood, so no matter how the Cowboys did, at least I won.

The game continued, more shots of guys milling around, more shots of cheerleaders, and then another two seconds of game. A commercial break interrupted the *action* with a preview of a new *Star Wars* series set to air next year.

Dad just about knocked over his plate reaching for the remote, and he switched to another channel. His face settled into the neutral frown he'd worn for the past six years. A hint of the sadness from before lingered in his eyes, which he kept fully engaged at the screen. His hand left the remote to hold his wallet.

The worm of guilt I spent the evening trying to ignore squirmed right back into my gut. He couldn't stand to watch a commercial that drug up memories, and there I went parading around in memory-fodder. He didn't use to have a problem with my six-oh activities, as long as I kept it far away from him, but recently I had to do more than keep it out of sight. He didn't want me doing it at all. Was it really just about the election?

The game resumed, and soon it was halftime. Dad got the ice cream and set both bowls on the tray between us. I spooned a big bite into my mouth, letting the cold soothe my throat, raw from too many convincing cheers.

"How was school?" Dad asked between bites.

I shrugged. "Good."

"Anything interesting going on?"

"Not really."

He clanked the spoon in his bowl and hefted a sigh. "Can you say more than two words, Son? I'm trying to have a conversation."

"'bout what?" I dug a peanut butter cup out of the ice cream. "Nothing to talk about at school, and you don't care about my hobbies."

"Pardon?" He sat upright in the recliner.

Why'd I say that out loud? His watchful gaze encompassed me like a security camera, and every flinch or move I made was huge. I avoided eye contact, focusing instead on the peanut chunks in my bowl.

Dad clicked his tongue. "Didn't we have a laugh on Mr. Pearson's boat last month?"

"Sure."

"Another damn one word answer. What's your problem?" He gestured, knocking the remote off his armrest.

My problem? He was the one who went mental because I wore a costume to a convention, a place where that's not only accepted but applauded. "Why can't I do stuff with the six-oh-second?"

He scoffed. "That why you're acting up?"

"No. But I wanna know the real reason."

"Told you." He leaned in the recliner, pushing the back so it tilted further. "I can't have my constituent base getting wind of your dress-up crap. What kind of respectable leader has his kid still doing that shit at your age? They'll question my judgment." He paused. "I'll lose votes."

My mouth hung open. Yeah, we had a lot of older folks in our area, but still. "That's nuts," I said.

Dad's relaxed posture began to stiffen, and his chest raised high with a huge breath. I felt the air blow out as he exhaled slowly. "You don't have to understand. I been in public office long enough to know." He shoved the handle of the recliner, cracking the footrest down, and stomped into the kitchen. A minute later, he returned with another beer for himself and a root beer for me.

He planted the bottle in my hand. "Watch the game."

For the rest of the second half, we went through the motions, and he accepted my apology for lying about the con. He didn't give me my phone or promise to pick up my car, so it didn't accomplish more than ease the ulcer, which was surely taking root in my stomach. After *we* won the game, I made my excuse and went back upstairs.

Though my room lived in a state of perpetual tidiness, I needed to do something, to fix something. I pressed the spines of each book on the shelf so they sat flush with one another and did the same with the video games and DVDs. My closet didn't need straightening. Everything put up in its place, the only thing I could control.

I sat at my desk and opened the laptop. Buzzing, the screen blinked and came to life. The threads I flagged in the six-oh's forum only received two new posts, both about where to find costuming supplies in small towns. I clicked the reply box, and then my speakers beeped.

Someone messaged me? I tabbed to the messenger.

JoshVader: Hey, you there?

Me: Yeah. What's up?

JoshVader: Where'd you go? You missed the Sunday wrap-up with the garrison.

I started to type what happened but deleted it.

Me: Family emergency. Had to leave. Sorry.

It was true enough. Josh's icon blinked that he was typing. The icon vanished for a minute, and then "typing" reappeared next to his name.

JoshVader: I hope all is OK.

Me: Thanks. Everything's fine. I'm good. Did you find my helmet at the lost and found?

JoshVader: No, sorry. I'll ship your stuff, though.

Me: Thanks.

JoshVader: See you at Dallas AniSuperCon in a few weeks?

Me: Maybe. I'll try.

JoshVader: Cool.

Wait, Josh had been the one who pointed out Audrey when she was looking for me. Maybe he talked to her.

Me: Do you remember that girl in the Sailor Moon costume?

JoshVader: Yeah, did you talk to her?

Me: Yup. Do you know her?

JoshVader: No. Just saw her that day. Why?

Me: Nevermind. Thanks tho.

He logged off shortly after, and that split second of optimism turned into a lead sheet draped over and shoving me into the floor. I had no way to speak with Audrey again. After I ran out of there like that, maybe she wouldn't want to. What did she think of me now?

The image of her cradling my phone zoomed into my mind. She had given me her number. She probably expected me to call her, and if I didn't…she'd think I was a jerk. If I could get my phone back, I'd at least text her. Dad could hold a grudge better than a scorned cheerleader; he wouldn't just give it back. How was I going to trick him into returning my phone?

8

Audrey

At around eight o'clock Sunday night, I shuffled through the front door. The rolling suitcase could keep the trunk warm for the night, because I sure as heck wasn't gonna lug that thing into the house. Maybe Dad would come out and get it for me.

I crossed the foyer and made a beeline for the kitchen, which smelled of vinegar and orange peels. The cleaning spray couldn't fully disguise the distinct cheesy aroma of whatever Mom had made for dinner. A silvery marble countertop separated the kitchen from the living room, but other than a change of tile to wood flooring, the whole area stretched into one big room.

Dad walked around the other side of the counter to join me in the kitchen. "You're back pretty late. Can't have Rick working you like a slave."

I grabbed a plate of enchiladas covered in cling wrap from the counter. The plate was still warm-ish. "I volunteered to help put things away at the store when we got back. Everything was a mess." He didn't need to know some of the merchandise got busted because I had a tantrum in the booth. Cleaning was the least I could do. "Oh, did Sara come home this weekend?"

Dad shook his head. "She had to study for exams, but she'll be home next weekend. Do you have another con?"

"Nope. Just work at the store." Maybe we could find the time to reconnect, a family movie or something. Sara had been preoccupied with her new friends, and I was always busy with work. If we actually spent some time together, we could act like sisters again. But, first things first. "I'm gonna eat in my room, okay?"

Mom called from the office, "Wash the plate when you're done. We don't need ants in the house." Disembodied-mom voice was pretty usual. She taught all day and then graded all night. Weekends I often spent road-tripping it with Uncle Rick. It was a miracle if we ever ate together.

"Okay!"

I took my plate and hopped upstairs into my room. It had been a long day, too long without a word. I had waited all day for the phone to ring, but it didn't even beep with a message. Kyle must know I was worried; he said he'd text. Could he? Was he okay? What really happened?

A quick internet search through the zillion Boba Fett cosplayers brought back Kyle's six-oh-second profile with zero info on it. He didn't even have a Facebook or Instagram account. What century did he live in?

Dan told me not to worry, but that was like asking me to stop breathing. He'd said he'd track down some way to contact Kyle. Because of the comic shop, Dan got into the con scene way earlier than me, and he knew many more cosplayers. He'd be able to find someone who knew Kyle.

I took out my phone and tapped a quick message.

Worried about Kyle. Can you ask Jake and Cora if they know anyone in his 602 group? Please reply soon. TY!

I waited. No response.

In the meantime, I ate a forkful of leftover enchiladas. Semi-warm, congealed cheesy goodness slid down my throat. Unfortunately, my happy stomach didn't lift my spirits. The silence from my phone left me numb. There was nothing more I could do.

I got up, took off my clothes, and tossed them to the floor by the closet. As I stepped into my violet PJ pants, I noticed a shirt lying in the heap. The half-naked elf chick folded into wrinkles on top of my jeans—Kyle's shirt. My heart skipped. I grabbed the shirt and held it to my chest, and though I was the first to wear it, I pretended it was really his. He had to be okay. Was he thinking of me, too?

The shirt didn't match at all. I put it back on anyway. I lifted the cherry blossom comforter and tried to get comfortable in bed. Pent-up energy made my limbs ache for movement. Exhaustion from the weekend weighed my eyelids, but my brain ran on overdrive. How could I ever sleep?

Kyle couldn't miss me like this, could he? We only just met. Heck, we hadn't even kissed or anything…but maybe we almost had. The image came fast, Kyle's face inches from mine, a dark hue running over his cheeks. Why didn't I see it then? Damn. What if I never saw him again?

The day after, Dan finally texted me back with "workin' on it," and then nothing else for the rest of the week. We didn't have any of the same electives, and he'd been disappearing during lunch. The school had opened off-campus lunch to seniors to ease lunchroom congestion, which meant Dan flaunted his Taco Bell and Carl's Jr. on a regular basis. Not this week. Why'd he go awol just when I needed him? He must know how important this was to me. At least I could catch him at work.

As soon as classes ended on Friday, I drove my old Corolla over to Uncle Rick's store and parked next to Dan's pickup with the missing tailgate. He beat me there? How many red light cameras snapped his license plate on the way over? And Mom said *I* had a lead foot.

The shopping strip looked pretty pathetic since the kids' consignment place closed up. Now there were two vacant storefronts, a Thai restaurant, a personal loan-shark office, and Uncle Rick's store on the corner.

Bells jingled when I opened the door, and behind the counter, Dan glanced to check who came in. He saw me across the empty store and returned to whatever he was messing with in the glass case.

"Hey, stranger." I walked over and used the register to clock in.

Dan set a few Zelda-inspired necklaces in the display and locked the case. "Hey."

"So?"

"So, what?" He flicked his gaze toward me and then out into the store. The edge of his mouth twitched. Gotcha.

"You found something." I shook his shoulder with a vice grip. "Did you find anything? A friend? His contact info?"

He gritted his teeth. I let go, and little indentions showed where my nails had dug into his shirt. "Damn, what if I hadn't found anything? I'm afraid for my life now," he said.

"Then you did?" I was so close to talking to Kyle again. I could feel it, like hope burrowing into my core.

Dan reached into his pocket and produced a crumpled Post-it note.

I took it from his fingertips. Blue Sharpie numbers in Dan's handwriting formed a near-legible phone number; the fives looked like S's.

No name or anything else. "Gonna tell me who to ask for? Is it a friend of his?"

He took a few seconds to get out the glass wipes. In slow, deliberate movements, he cleaned the case, removing each of his fingerprints from the glass. The dork wanted to kill me with anticipation. It was working.

"Dan!"

"Chillax," he said. "I thought you knew his name. Kyle, wasn't it?"

That seed of hope blossomed into a freakin' sunflower, ready to burst out of my chest. "What?" I wet my mouth. "How'd you find it?"

By now, Dan had scrubbed the glass into sparkling submission, but he kept at it as he spoke. "On the six-oh-second website I found a picture with him and a cosplayer Cora knows, Josh Hartman. She asked him for his friend's house number. No biggie."

"Yes, it is!" I wrapped my arms around his shoulders, squeezing them to his sides in the most intense rib-crushing hug I could manage.

"Ox—" He gasped. "Oxygen."

I let go, and he exaggerated his near-death experience by bending over the counter and heaving.

"How can I ever thank you?" I asked.

Dan shrugged. He grabbed the container of wipes and put them in the cabinet under the cash register, his back to me again.

"I mean it. I owe you big time."

"Okay, you wanna do something for me?"

"Anything," I said.

He turned and looked straight at my face, something he hadn't done since I walked in. "Go out with me."

"What?" The word bubbled up my throat like a burp, unstoppable.

For a second, he might have looked hurt, but his wry smile returned right away. He'd played jokes on me since we were kids, water balloon ambushes and lies about putting orange juice in my chocolate milk. Of course he'd do this to me now. The worst possible timing, because he knew I liked Kyle.

I opened my mouth, and he said, "Sunday, you pay for lunch. I'll order something outrageous. We'll be even."

"Sure," I said. Was it really just about the money? He seemed normal now, but that look he had...

Behind us, the door to the stockroom slammed open. Uncle Rick backed in with his arms full of two cardboard boxes. "A little help?"

I jumped and grabbed the top box, which had almost fallen. I placed it on the counter, and Uncle Rick carried the other to the comics rack against the wall. He opened it up, glanced at the door—silent and still, as always—and heaved a sigh.

"Audrey?" He waved me over.

I left Dan, which was fine with me, and went to help Uncle Rick unpack the comics. I grabbed a bundle, and he put his hand on mine.

He cleared his throat. "I know it's awful to do this to you, but can you take your pay in merchandise again? I promise I'll have enough for your paycheck next time."

"Don't worry about it," I said.

"I hate doing this to you, hun." He moved his hand and let me put the comics on the display.

I smiled. "I don't mind. I'd probably spend half my paycheck at the store anyway." Because of the discount, I did spend a stupid amount of money on DVDs and graphic novels, but not as much as I'd gotten recently. Uncle Rick had enough stress about the shop without me whining that I wanted a real check.

Though, my account was getting thin, and tomorrow I'd have to buy Dan a lobster or something. Maybe he'd go easy on me. Right, if it was really about the money, I'd be paying for a deluxe meal for sure. It was worth it whatever the cost. I reached into my pocket and felt the folded edges of the Post-it note. I'd buy a hundred lobsters for that little piece of paper. I had Kyle's number, and now all I had to do was drum up the courage to dial it.

Kyle

Someone knocked on the classroom door. "Hey, you done yet? Band finished practice fifteen minutes ago." Since Garrett had to come in on Saturdays anyway, I'd begged him for a ride home after tutoring. At least I could make money without access to my car.

I nodded. "Yeah, we're done."

My student zipped his backpack and trotted through the door. I only brought a graphing calculator, which I dropped into my duffel with the JROTC stuff. I took the uniform off right after our meeting in the morning; no reason to wear it longer than necessary.

Garrett held the door open. "Hurry up, man. I've got a date tonight."

"And you need three hours to get some plastic surgery?"

He knocked me against the door frame as I walked by, and a sting shot up my bruised shoulder. I grabbed my arm.

"Sorry man. I didn't mean to hit you that hard." He adjusted his backpack and continued into the hall. Thankfully he hadn't made a big deal out of nothing. Dad might've been a touch rough getting me in the truck, but he meant well. Mostly. He could stand to back off and let me be.

"S'okay, I asked for it. I'll refrain from joking on date nights, since you're so prone to violence."

Garrett snickered. "Yeah, yeah. Tell that to my fellow clarinetists, and maybe I can bluff my way to first chair."

We left the empty classroom and passed a few students who were heading to weekend activities. The building itself was like a body, and students flowed through its veins as blood. Sometimes the heart beat slow, the population within the halls dwindling to a trickle…but never empty. I got to see the school at all different times, from the vigorous pulse of day to the sleepy current of evening. Maybe the heart stopped in the dead of night. Too bad I had to eventually go home, or I could make it live on my own.

The drive went way too fast, and I closed Garrett's car door in time to see Dad pull into the garage. I hurried up the front steps and into the house, my friend gone before I turned the key. As I locked the door behind me, footsteps sounded from the utility room entrance.

Dad dropped his briefcase by the hutch in the foyer. "Why're you home so late?"

He asked that instead of *how* I got back? "Tutoring."

"Oh, right." He turned the corner into the kitchen, but continued talking through the wall like I should be able to hear him.

I followed, the beeps of the preheated oven signaling another frozen delicacy for dinner. "What'd you say, Dad?"

"Which pizza you want?" He opened the freezer.

"Supreme if we have the kind without green olives." Why'd they always put those things on there?

"Got the good brand, only black ones." Dad readied a pizza, per usual. He'd cook steaks or one of those skillet things if he got home early enough. He never did. Some law offices had family friendly hours, but Dad stopped getting those when he got promoted, weekends especially. Apparently partners had to pull more weight or prove to one another they could work the longest, like some kind of litigious pissing contest. Add the city council meetings on top of that, and we had a sure-fire recipe for frozen "home cooking."

I left the kitchen behind to go to my room and relax in my own space for however long it'd take to cook. I set the duffel on the bed and grabbed my laptop from the desk.

From down the hall, the home phone rang. Dad picked up to deal with the solicitors, but I didn't hear his usual diatribe about fraudulent charity companies.

"Kyle," he yelled, "Hurry and get the phone!"

Who could be calling me? I ran, more like flew, down the hall to the bonus room and picked up the extra handset. "Got it!"

I heard a hang-up beep and exhaled. "Hello?"

"Kyle?" The feminine voice sounded a little scared…and familiar.

Could it be? "Audrey?"

"Please don't think I'm crazy or stalking you or something, but I was worried after what happened, and then you didn't call—not that you had to or whatever. Anyway, my friend got your number from Josh, and I just wanted to see if you were okay." She mumbled something after that.

All the colors in the world around me muted, and the only thing that mattered was the voice on the other end of the phone. "Aud—"

"I'm sorry. I probably should have waited."

"Hey, hey, s'okay." I smiled, though she couldn't see. "Thank you."

"For what?" Her breath hitched at the end.

I couldn't speak for a minute as a surge of something gripped my chest. "For, for calling. Dad took my phone, or I woulda texted. I swear." Was this really happening? Did she actually call me?

"So, *are* you okay?" Audrey seemed so worried. I could almost picture her wide, shimmering eyes, which made the whole humiliation worth it.

"Much better now."

"I'm glad," she said.

"Sorry our date got cut short though. I was having fun." *Having fun, who says that? Holy crap, did I just say "date?"* My gut flip-flopped, rolled over, and died.

"Me too." She didn't hesitate. "I hope we can meet up again sometime."

The oversized clock ticked past another minute. Our call had a limit because when that pizza finished, I'd have to go. If Dad connected this call to the convention, to my cosplay, he could weird-out on me again. My insides seized. Too much to say and not enough time. "Do you have a piece of paper? I'll give you my email and number, so whenever I get that back we can talk longer."

"Yeah." Rustling echoed over the phone. "Got it."

I only signed up for an email so I could create my six-oh and shopping accounts, but now I'd have a reason to check it. I gave her the details, and she told me her number, too. We wouldn't be stuck incommunicado again. By now the pizza had to be nearly finished, which meant Dad might pick up the phone and figure out who I was talking to.

"What about AniSuperCon, you going to that?" Audrey asked.

"My car's been abandoned at the hotel, so I'm kinda stranded here."

"What?"

I sighed. That did sound overkill, didn't it. "Yeah. It's not as bad as it sounds, though. A friend drives me home from school."

A long pause followed, and then she asked, "What school do you go to?"

"Waco High," I said. "Why?"

"Waco? Wow. But…doable. I need to figure some stuff out. I'll send you an email later, okay?"

"Okay."

Four extra-loud beeps came from the kitchen. Not enough time, never enough. "Sorry Audrey, gotta go. We'll talk later, right?"

"Of course. Later…Kyle."

The phone clicked, and a dial tone replaced her voice. The way she said my name sent a warm tingle over my skin, and I'd give anything I had to hear her say it. I'd have a chance to; we both promised. She even had some plan. Though, why'd she need to know where I went to school? Whatever, as long as it meant I'd see her again. Maybe I'd get to see her again.

10

Audrey

Dan's voice echoed in my head, *go out with me*. It sounded so serious, but right afterward he laughed about squeezing my wallet for all it was worth. He hadn't meant a real date. Besides, we grew up together; he may as well be my brother.

I paused outside the Texas Road Ho, what we called the Roadhouse ever since the summer when the back-half of the sign had burned out, and checked my phone. I swiped over to my bank app and took a peek, fifty-five dollars. As long as I kept twenty in there, they wouldn't charge me a minimum balance fee. Maybe I could get a side salad as an entree or something.

The hostess guided me past a butcher case in the foyer, filled with raw steaks the size of my head, and up a ramp into the restaurant. Peanut shells crunched under my sneakers. Classy as a circus.

After sliding into the wooden booth, Dan handed me a laminated menu from the condiment box against the window.

"And this was your top pick?" I asked over the whining from the toddler in the next booth.

He waved his menu at me. "I can get a twenty-ounce ribeye for half the price of a fancy steak place and just as much flavor. I wanted you to treat me, not drain your account."

"That's considerate of you."

"Chivalry is my middle name." Dan ripped a roll in half and smeared a huge glob of cinnamon butter through the middle. He shoved the whole thing in his mouth, which puffed out his cheeks like a squirrel. Yup, gentleman all the way.

I glanced at the price next to that steak he mentioned, not exorbitant, but not cheap either. "I think you need a new dictionary."

It took him another minute to swallow his mouthful of bread-butter sandwich. "I'll go edit the Wikipedia entry when I get home. That count?"

I snickered. "Marginally."

The waitress dropped by, and our orders came through pretty fast. Dan didn't act any different than usual. He ate his enormous steak, while I speared some ranch-covered lettuce pretending I was on a diet. As long as I tipped light, I'd stay above the minimum balance. No problem. Getting gas money might be a challenge.

When I finished my piddly salad, I snacked on more of the free rolls, which tasted better than most of the food on the menu.

"And then Dad accidentally ordered twelve dozen dolls, instead of just twelve. They let him make a return though." Dan shook his head. "If he doesn't figure out how to use a website on his own, I'll die."

"Yeah." I slid the breadbasket across the table so they wouldn't tempt me with their buttery goodness. "Oh, website, that reminds me. I haven't told you what happened after you got me Kyle's number. I called last night, and can you believe his dad took his phone. That's why he didn't text."

Dan shoved a forkful of mashed potatoes in his mouth.

I continued, "And, get this, his dad was the one who took him at the hotel. He abandoned his car. It's been in the garage since the con. He has no idea when—"

"Just stop, okay." Dan dropped his fork on the table with a *clank*. "What?"

He gazed at his mostly empty plate. "Can we not talk about him?"

"You helped me find him. I thought you'd want to know…"

"I don't."

"Why?" I asked.

Dan looked up from his plate, his mouth turned down. It was so weird to see a frown on him. "You just said the guy's got an insane father. You barely know him, and you don't need to have that kind of crap in your life. Just drop it and move on."

"You know I can't."

He smacked the table with his palm, and water splashed out of our glasses. Cold drops rained onto my arm.

My jaw dropped. "Why are you acting like this?"

"You're so dense sometimes!" Dan spat. "Figure it out." He yanked a twenty from his wallet and tossed it on the table. He pushed past a waitress, disappearing out the front door into the night outside. The tension had blocked the noise, but now the clatter from the kitchen and the hanging TVs filled an empty space around me.

I couldn't leave, twenty didn't cover the check, and I'd have to wait for the server to run my debit card. Stares and whispers focused in from the other patrons who'd witnessed the scene. It must have looked like my boyfriend ditched me after a fight. They couldn't know the truth, that Dan wasn't…

His angry glare came back to me. Not angry, hurt. Dense barely scratched the surface, because the whole world—the restaurant patrons included—saw what I'd missed for a long while now. Dan wasn't just the boy I grew up with anymore.

On my way home, I blasted the *Marmalade Boy* soundtrack through open windows. Driving took some focus, and the lyrics took the rest as I sang along in butchered Japanese. Soon I arrived in my room. A lamp brightened the corner behind the desk, fabric anime scrolls covering most of the mint-green walls. I was surrounded by exuberant faces and bright colors, but that slick feeling stuck to me like oil. I couldn't ignore it away, and the more I thought about anything else, the more it clung tight.

How long had Dan thought of me like that?

How much had I hurt him?

Did he hate me now?

Without urging, the thoughts returned, pounding a rock in my stomach with a hammer. What could I have done differently? Maybe I shouldn't have prattled on so much about Kyle. I loved Dan, just not the way he wanted.

Someone had to get hurt.

"Aaah!" I squeezed a stuffed cat pillow until its ears rounded like balloons. I threw it onto the bed with a sigh.

Ba-deep!

I checked my phone. A new message? No, it was an email that wasn't spam. Kyle replied. The excitement washed out everything that came before, and with a trembling finger, I tapped it open.

Hi. Things are okay here. My schedule doesn't have much free time. Tuesdays and Thursdays I stay till 7:00 tutoring. It pays pretty well. I wanna go to AniSuperCon to see you. I'll come up with something. Have a good night.

Oh, this is Kyle.

The message appeared as text on a small glowing screen, but I heard his voice clear as day. Even the "good night" sounded like he had a twinge of nerves about ending the message, or of not knowing what to say. Maybe it was the flutters in my heart making me think it, but either way, it was cute.

Tomorrow Kyle would be at school until about seven. That'd give us plenty of time to drive up to Dallas to get his car, and for him to turn around and get home without suspicion. I could leave during my teacher aide period and surprise him right after class; he'd freak.

A giggle slipped out as I typed my reply, short and sweet.

See you tomorrow.

I hit send, and not three seconds later, my phone beeped again.

His reply: *What?*

I could picture it now, his jaw slack and brows tied together as he puzzled through what it meant. Oh, I couldn't wait to see his face. I'd drive down there and find…oh no, the drive. It'd take well over an hour. I didn't have enough gas, and if I filled my tank, I'd overdraw my account.

How could I make it all the way there and back on a quarter tank? If I got Mom's credit card, I could fill up. She only used that card for gas and car service anyway. She shouldn't mind me borrowing it.

Darkness had replaced the usual sliver of light beneath the door. Silent as a rogue nailing a stealth roll, I cracked the door and tiptoed down the stairs. Mom's purse lay where it always did, on the counter separating the kitchen and living room. I took the card out of the wallet.

The fridge closed quickly, salad dressing and condiment containers clinking together. I dropped the wallet in the purse and jumped back into the living room.

Sara stepped further into the kitchen. The neighbor's floodlights streamed in through the blinds, so I could see her face in stripes.

"What are you doing in Mom's purse?" She held a bottle of cola, her blonde hair trailing over her back, instead of in a ponytail.

I forgot how to talk as I stared at my sister, who graced me with her presence at the worst possible time. Then it hit me. "Wait. What are you doing home? It's a weeknight. Don't you have class tomorrow?"

"Tuesdays start late for me, and I came home for dinner with Mom and Dad. This isn't about me." She gestured her soda toward the counter and the purse.

"Borrowing a few bucks for gas." I shoved the card into my jeans. "I'll replace it when I get paid."

If I ever got paid.

Sara frowned exactly like Mom. "Stealing? Audrey, that's not like you."

"Borrowing." I crossed my arms in front of my chest, and the irritation about her abandoning me at the store flooded forward as if it had happened seconds ago. She liked avoiding me, so why couldn't she do it now? "I'm sure you can keep quiet about it. You're good at that."

"What do you mean?" She twisted open her bottle. The *hiss* of carbonation sounded like an alarm.

"You know."

She had the bottle to her lips, but shifted it down so she could speak. "No. I don't." She sighed. "What's going on with you? You're taking Mom's credit card and acting...I don't even know."

And there Sara went, trying to play mother hen at home, when in public she barely acknowledged that I breathed. Oh no, she probably thought she was *responsible* for me too, which would mean she'd have to keep me from making her look bad. She could end up saying something to ease her conscience.

"Please." I slid my bare foot back and forth against the wood floor. "Don't tell Mom I borrowed the money."

"More than a few bucks?"

"Yeah."

Sara gulped her soda and took a minute to look me down. "Okay. I won't tell Mom."

A rush of air hit my lungs. Maybe I'd misjudged her? "Really?"

Sara nodded, and I think a little frown tugged her perfect smile down, only for a split-second. "You're my sister. But, you have to promise you'll pay her back. It is just for gas after all."

"Thank you." I didn't know what else to say. Even if Sara pretended she was an only child outside the house, at least at home, she could be a real sister.

She shrugged and disappeared upstairs, where I should follow. I waited until her footsteps retreated to the end of the hall and into her room. Would Sara keep her word? Mom might not get mad about a few dollars, but she'd probably be pissed if I didn't ask to borrow her credit card. Asking left room for her to say no, and it was better to beg forgiveness after the fact. Because afterward, I'd have already met up with Kyle. Getting grounded then would sting a whole lot less.

Kyle

Tutoring algebra was a pretty easy gig, and I certainly didn't mind the extra time out of the house. One of my earliest students, Eric, sat at a desk facing mine in the empty classroom. He pulled out his book and a folder full of practice problems. Midway through the first sheet, he looked up, training his twisted brows on something behind me.

I craned my neck toward the door, and someone was standing right by the chalkboard—Audrey. She held my Boba Fett helmet between her hands like it was made of glass.

"Wha?" I flailed as my chair tipped back, and I banged my knee into the underside of the desk. "Ow!" By shifting my weight, I somehow kept the chair upright.

"Are you okay?" Audrey appeared at my side, glancing under the desk to see me rub my knee in a vain attempt to make it better.

I tried to force an even tone. "Fine. I'm fine."

"I didn't even get to say 'surprise.'" She held out the helmet, and I took hold of the sides, just below her hands. Our fingers touched as she released it into my grip.

Her wicked grin widening, she backed a step away from the desk. Instead of a costume or that black T-shirt, she wore boot-cut jeans and a tank in a pale blue-green color. The color probably had a name, seafoam or puce or some crazy name they give paint that I'd never recognize. Whatever it was, it made her deep brown eyes glow, and the fabric hugged her—

"Kyle?" Eric waved his hand in front of my eyes.

I shook my head and looked at Eric instead of where I'd been staring, which, oh no. "Sorry, yeah." Wait a second. I turned to Audrey. "How did you? What're you doing here?"

"How? Well, I had to ask around, and a student aide pointed me this way for tutoring." She lifted her chin. "Why? I came to help you get your car home of course."

"Really?"

Audrey nodded, and in the desk opposite me, Eric moved in his chair. Oh crud.

I said, "I've got a student…"

Eric slid his folder into the backpack on the floor. "Don't worry about it. I think I have this stuff anyway."

"Your test is Thursday."

He shrugged. "I can meet tomorrow if you can. It's more important to get your car back, right?" The freshman winked, swinging his pack over his shoulder. *Did he really just wink at me?*

I scrambled out from the desk and handed Eric his water bottle. "Do you know Brian Wall? I was fixing to meet him next."

"Sure, I'll tell him something came up."

"Just don't mention that 'something' is a cute girl." I flinched, noticing Audrey's ears turn purple. "I mean, my car. Tell him about the car."

Eric took a swig from his water. His cheeks puffed more than they should've. "I've got you covered." He capped his drink and left us alone.

Audrey leaned against a desk, her hands gripping the edge. She was really there, here…in my school. I was holding my Boba Fett helmet in a classroom. Audrey, the six-oh, school, and reality—they existed at the same time in the same moment, overlapping time and space. Conventions seemed like some kind of pocket dimension, but now my fantasy blurred into real life. All of that had actually happened, and more important, she drove all the way here for me. Just for me.

A full minute passed before I realized the magnitude of the awkward silence, and now I had to breech it. "You…you're here."

Stating the obvious, excellent start.

She drummed her fingers on the bottom of the desk. "I know I should've warned you, but I thought at the time that it'd be a fun surprise. If you can't go to Dallas, I understand."

"No, no no no! I'm going. I wanna go." I walked over, shoved the helmet in the crook of my arm, reached for one of her fidgeting hands.

She released her grip on the desk, sliding her palm between my fingers.

I squeezed. "It's a good surprise. And, thank you." Tutoring was supposed to last until the evening, so Dad wasn't expecting me home soon anyway. If I got back a little late, the frozen lasagna could keep warm in the oven. No big deal.

The uncertainty vanished from her voice, and she yanked me toward the door. "I'm in the visitor lot so they don't ticket me. Let's go."

We half-jogged through the hallways, giving life to the slowing ebb of the after-school rush. A minute later we were already buckling in. Audrey pulled out of the parking lot onto the road.

I had to give Audrey directions through town to avoid the traffic circle downtown (a certifiable death trap), and after a few more turns, we sped up the ramp to the interstate. Familiar gas stations and strip malls zipped by until the highway stretched into a flat nothing north of Waco. Orange traffic barrels lined the corridor of perpetual construction, but we had luck making good time anyway.

Audrey tapped her fingers on the steering wheel. "What's it like living outside the Metroplex?"

"S'okay, I guess. We probably got all the same retail you do. Not much different."

"Looks like the stuff out here has more character. Plus, you're close to the country, so it's safer in emergencies."

I chuckled. "The online zombie survival quiz does give me extra points for it."

"My backup zombie apocalypse scenario was to go north toward Oklahoma, but maybe coming here would be a better bet." She smiled.

"Damn, now I kinda wanna face the undead."

"I'll get my bug-out bag ready to go." She didn't miss a beat. It's like we shared a resonance connecting our thoughts, right from one head to the other.

That was only the beginning. We talked about the con and recent Marvel movies, and by the time we reached the edge of downtown, we'd discussed everything from comfort food favorites—brisket for her, fried okra for me—to the likelihood of the AI singularity happening within our lifetimes.

The same drive on the way home with Dad had taken a million years in deafening silence, but with Audrey it ended too soon. Most of the time, I had to focus on tutoring, JROTC, homework, or making sure things went smoothly at home. I'd direct the conversation away from bad topics, keep Dad happy. I didn't have space to talk to someone about random stuff, about everything really. I didn't have to walk on eggshells with Audrey. I could just…be.

Skyscrapers blocked the blinding sun from the west, and time crunched into an ever-shrinking ball of… something that shrinks. We were almost there. Then it'd all be over. I'd have to drive home, alone.

Audrey exited the highway and turned onto the surface street toward the hotel and the only free garage nearby. "And I had to explain to Uncle Rick what a MEME is. How do you explain that? It just *is*, ya know?"

The clicking of the turn signal ticked loud like a clock. "Yeah."

"What's wrong?"

"Nothing," I lied.

She drove the car into the empty parking garage, which made it all the easier to zero in on my lone car parked below a pillar. She pulled up beside it.

I gazed out the window at my run-down sedan, still mostly blue. The thing worked better than it looked, and I'd always been grateful to have it. Now I had it back, thanks to her. Garrett, or any of my JROTC friends, never even thought to drag me here. She did. And she asked for nothing in return. I never met anyone so kind before, so beautiful. Amazing.

A nagging voice in the back of my head said that Dad would be worried if I came home late, but Audrey. Amazing Audrey. The current of energy from the first time we met had strengthened into a voltage needing a warning sign, and it had more than enough power to muffle any thought that wasn't about her.

I said, "I don't wanna go home yet."

Audrey's hand gripped the key, but she didn't turn it off. "We did make great time."

"Could get some dinner." I added, "My treat."

Audrey shifted into drive. "There's one of those build-your-own burrito places on the next block." She peeled out of the garage and straight to the restaurant.

This time we had a real date, eating food while sitting in chairs, the whole nine yards. I even paid, which Audrey seemed more than mildly grateful for. The tutor gig had to pay a higher rate than her uncle's comic store. I'd spend every cent if it meant I could stay with her longer.

Audrey must have had the same thought, and we ate our burritos in tiny bites, waiting in-between, and sipping on our Cokes. We camped in those uncomfortable metal chairs for long-past the socially acceptable time to hang in a fast-food joint. After the manager asked us if we "needed anything" for the third occasion, we cleared the table and left.

In another nanosecond, we were parked next to my car again. I didn't make a move to leave, and Audrey didn't ask me to. The evening took on more of that dream-like quality. Was any of this real? Did I really meet this remarkable girl who drug my butt all the way from Waco just to pick up my car?

When I turned, she was looking my direction, whether at me or zoning out I couldn't tell. The poor lighting in the garage darkened her face, but the reflection of her blue-ish shirt lit her eyes from underneath. She wore the lip glitz stuff again. Heat filled my head, and a pressure shook in my chest.

A wave of bravery belonging to someone else took my arm and squeezed her against me. Her warm body relaxed instead of tensing, and my pulse acted like I'd run the mile in four seconds.

Audrey watched me back through half-lidded eyes, and her sparkly lips parted enough that I could hear a slight quickening to her breath. The nerves I had before—gone. I leaned in and kissed her, letting my right hand brush past her cheek and tangle into the hair at the nape of her neck. Soft and just a little sticky, her lips tasted like strawberry fruit snacks.

Her hands pressed into my shoulder blades, and she kissed me back. Every nerve in my body tingled.

Audrey's phone chimed, which interrupted the moment. She pulled back for a second, and I caught a glance at the clock. Oh, shit. I sat up straight, and she startled.

She sucked in her bottom lip. "What's wrong?"

"Oh man, I need to get home."

"Traffic might suck, but a few minutes won't make a difference," she said.

I shook my head. "My dad's gonna be worried."

"Worried? He doesn't seem the type." Her voice came out a little harsh.

"What's that supposed to mean?"

"He's why we're here in the first place. He abandoned your car! Doesn't that sound insane?" Audrey shifted further into the driver's seat, away from me.

The sudden awareness of exactly how late I'd be getting home hit like a punch to the gut, and a wave of unease raised goose bumps all over my skin. *I've been gone too long. What if he's looking for me?* The clock on the dash ticked past another minute. "I should probably go."

Audrey took a black thingie from the console and tied her hair in a ponytail. "Why do you care what he thinks? What kind of parent treats their kid that way?" She looked back at me again. "I'm worried about you."

The creased photo wormed into my brain, the one Dad carried in his wallet. "My dad loves me, just gotta warped way of showing it since my mom died."

She gasped. "Oh, no. I'm so sorry…" She reached across and let her fingers gently rest over the top of my hand between the seats.

I twisted my wrist so we could lace our fingers together. "S'okay. Happened when I was in third grade—ALS. I mean, the doctors prepared us for it and everything. Wasn't a surprise."

"Still, it's sad. I'm sorry." She sat quiet for a second, but then asked. "You seem normal though. Why'd it make your dad act like that?"

I tried to sound neutral. "Yeah. Seems like a long time for me, but I dunno, must be different for him. Maybe seeing her get worse and worse was hard on him. Afterward, Dad was just sad, and at first he tried extra hard at the parenting thing. Helped with my band stuff, supported me, and all that jazz. But eventually he got too involved. Like, he dictated what activities I had to join. I think…I think he wanted me to 'turn out good' for Mom's memory."

"But freaking out over cosplay?" She cocked her brow.

"He used to be mostly okay with my six-oh stuff as long as I didn't flaunt it. *Star Wars* was Mom's thing, and I got into it when I was little. When she died, it felt like every book I read or every game I played brought me closer to her. Though the six-oh is my homage, Dad doesn't get it."

Audrey nodded. "That's beautiful."

"Thanks." I squeezed her hand. "He's gotten weirder about the cosplay stuff now. There's a reelection coming up for the city council, and he says pictures of me on the internet can hurt his campaign. Think that's bull, but whatever."

"You're not hurting his election. He's nuts."

I unhooked my fingers from hers and clasped my hands in my lap. "He's not crazy. He's depressed sometimes, and I get that."

Shifting upright in her seat, Audrey broke eye contact. "I guess you'll do what he wants then. I wanted to see you again, but if—"

"Hey, hey what?" I turned toward her. "I want to see you, too. You know I do."

"I work a lot of cons, and that's where I have free time."

The way she looked at me with those shimmering eyes released me from an intangible hold. I couldn't throw away a chance with Audrey because Dad had some ludicrous notion that I was gonna damage his campaign. Nothing I said or did would matter to the people who vote. Whatever he didn't know wouldn't hurt him.

"I'll see you at AniSuperCon?" I asked.

"You're going?"

The energy from before still with me, I said, "I wouldn't miss it if the zombie horde was knocking down my door."

Dad's car sat in the still-open garage when I pulled into the driveway more than an hour after Garrett was due to drop me off. On the drive, I'd rehearsed my story over and over, but standing at the front door, it disappeared from my brain like crashing hard drive. Maybe Dad wouldn't ask?

Crossing through the doorway, I expected the smell of freezer lasagna, but it wasn't there. The oven hadn't been on. Stillness claimed the dim living room and darkened kitchen, with only the hall light as evidence Dad had come home at all. The weird unease slid back like a second skin, wrapping all around me and making my heart race.

I went inside and immediately put my backpack in the coat closet. Dad's Marines cap fell, and I tossed it back onto the shelf, before closing the closet door. Taking a deep breath, I jogged up the stairs. The light from the office beamed under the doorway.

"Dad?" I cracked the door.

Hunching over the desk, Dad held the phone to his ear with one shoulder as he typed into a spreadsheet. "Yes, yes I know. Of course that's why they chose our firm, so I'm getting this case from the city council side, too. They want one down here and one in Dallas, and they think if they win us over, they can take both."

Papers littered the desk in a complete mess. My fingers itched to organize it, but I couldn't intrude.

He tensed while listening to the phone, shoulders bunched higher and tighter. From behind he looked like a boulder. "The board is split, but being the lead on the case, my argument will be stronger. If Waco lets one in for revenue, the Dallas option will follow suit." He paused. "Yes, okay. Set up a meeting tomorrow. See you then."

Dad clicked off the phone and spun around in his chair. "I called your friend Garrett. He said you weren't at tutoring. Did you know I near called the police? There's a few officers from city hall, even got Karl's number in my phone."

"Sorry," I muttered. "Didn't think—"

"No, you didn't." He stood up, suddenly a thousand feet tall, and the wrinkles creasing his forehead doubled the weight crushing me. I couldn't name the sensation, a rattling inside that made me want to run away and make things better all at once.

"Where have you been?" he yelled.

A glob filled my throat, making me croak. "I…I um…my car. Another friend took me to get my car."

Dad's jaw cracked loud enough for me to hear. "What?"

Get a grip, Kyle! I breathed out my nose. "I know you don't have time, so my friend took me. Hope that's okay."

"You went clear up to Dallas today? Without calling?" His anger morphed into a wide open mouth. His chest heaved with rapid breaths, and even a child could tell something had scared him. I had scared him.

"I'm sorry. Didn't have my phone, and I don't know your number without it." I backed up to the doorway, my spine hitting the frame.

Dad's intimidating stature curled forward, a deep frown overtaking his face. "Shit, you know how those yuppies drive—you can't swing a dead cat without hitting a five car pileup. What if something had happened? What if you'd gotten hit?"

Why'd I do something so dumb? We already lost Mom…of course he'd be worried about me. "I'm sorry," I said again.

He put his hand on his chest like he wanted to hold his heart and stop its obvious reaction. "Don't do that to me again."

The unnamed rattling in my body cleared into a lead ball of guilt. I was such an ass. "I won't."

With a heavy sigh, Dad walked past me into the hall. I followed him down the stairs into the living room where he went over to the fireplace. He reached into a little bowl on the mantel. "Suppose it's my fault for confiscating your phone. Don't go anywhere without asking first."

That's where he kept it, this whole time?

He tossed—more like pitched—the phone to me. I barely caught it before it hit the floor I tried to say thank you, but my mouth clamped tight. Thank you sounded weird in response to screwing up so badly, and apologizing again could invite the rage back. So, I silently nodded, awkwardly holding the phone at my side.

"I couldn't eat, but you can heat up something. I've got to get back to work." He offered a weak smile and lumbered over to the stairs.

As if I could eat now either. I waited until I heard the office door close, then hurried up the stairs into my room. The lump in my gut didn't disappear. How'd things change so quickly? A couple hours before, I had a date…kissed Audrey. Nothing could've taken me off of that high, but Dad had. It was tainted.

I lifted the phone and clicked on the screen. Audrey's number appeared on the contact list. She put it there with her own soft hands, and now her voice was only a phone call away. I got my car back, too. Nothing bad had happened, and eventually Dad would calm down. Things were looking up after all. The phone made me feel like I'd reclaimed something more significant than the collection of circuits and plastic. I held it in my palm, its slight weight a symbol of freedom.

12

Audrey

If I sped through a dozen red lights on the way home, I wouldn't have noticed. One second Kyle was kissing me, and the next I had already gotten out of the car. The entire drive went on autopilot while I relived those moments, breaking them into individual seconds, and feeling his lips, his hand on my neck, his strong shoulders…everything. Everything but the last minute or so. He was weirdly protective of his dad, the same dad that literally dragged him out of the con. No matter what Kyle said, that wasn't normal. At least he was probably okay at home.

Probably.

As I hurried through the threshold, dishes clinked in the rhythm of someone loading the dishwasher. The smell of burnt mozzarella hit my nose. A knot lodged into my stomach like I had actually eaten some of the family casserole. I had missed dinner again.

Dad sat in the recliner and Sara lounged sideways on the sofa, taking up all three cushions. She was home tonight? A spark hit me with giddiness. We could talk like we used to, and this time *I'd* have a boy to gush about. Maybe she'd let me borrow clothes or share secrets or give me dating tips. If she saw me as a normal girl, I'd lose that nerdy little-sister label, and she'd hang out with me, ya know, outside the house.

"Hey." I walked over to the sofa.

Dad clicked the remote from one news channel to another. "Leftovers are in the fridge if you haven't eaten."

"Thanks, Dad." I looked down at Sara, who was tapping furiously on her phone. "Sara?"

"One sec." The glow lit her face in pale white, her eyes in a zombie-esque stare.

My fingers pulled at the edge of my shirt. I waited. "Hey, so, you're actually home on a weeknight again. I thought we could—"

She held up a hand. "Stop, I'm replying to someone."

"Who's more important than me," I muttered.

Sara either didn't hear or didn't care, because she continued to text her friend instead of spend two seconds listening to her sister. Dad had gotten sucked into the news story about flooding streets. Who knew invisibility was such an easy skill to master.

I slipped past them and up the stairs. So what if Sara didn't care or didn't want to hear about Kyle. I wanted to relive the moment, bask in the glow, even if I had to on my own. Nobody was going to ruin my after-date rush, so I put everyone but Kyle out of my mind. I went to my room to return to my glorious daydream, which was actually honest-to-God reality. I had a boyfriend, a cute boyfriend with gray-blue eyes the color of the sky over the ocean. Not only did Kyle *get* me, but he was so thoughtful, maybe too thoughtful, and he had a smile that could tear down any self-conscious worry in a heartbeat.

I sat in my desk chair and spun in circles until it slowed to a stop, leaving me dizzy in front of a blank monitor. Blinking a few times brought me back to myself. I flicked the screen on to see my opened email and calendar. Two weekends away, the teal highlighted entry read "AniSuperCon!!!" My finally calm heart skipped one last beat. I'd see him then.

Wouldn't it be amazing if we could cosplay as a couple? Of course, I only had one real costume, Sailor Moon. I'd never ask Kyle to don a Tuxedo Kamen getup, even if he'd look hot in a top hat and billowing silk-lined cape. It'd be easy; just go to a tux rental place like they use for weddings. My face burned with the thought, and I shook my head. No, I couldn't. It was too girly.

Kyle didn't need to cosplay something for me. After all, he did *Star Wars* to honor his mom. He was so committed that he made it six-oh-second regulation, which wasn't cheap. Maybe I could do something like that, too. I could join the six-oh, connect with him…impress him.

I opened a new tab, the cursor blinking in the empty field. Who should I dress as? Boba Fett didn't have any female accomplice to match him, but what about other bounty hunters?

That's it! The idea flew right to my fingertips, and Google images brought back hundreds of pictures of Princess Leia in bounty hunter garb from when she rescued Han. The whole thing couldn't be more on target.

The pants and boot covers wouldn't be expensive, and I could repurpose a cheap gi from a martial arts dojo for the top. Getting Worbla for the shoulder armor and finding the helmet would be tricky though. Well not tricky, expensive. The con was only two weeks away, and dust was already settling on the empty vault floor of my imaginary bank account.

It was wrong, so wrong, but my hand wiggled into my pocket to retrieve Mom's credit card. Sara had overreacted before. It wasn't stealing. I only planned to borrow the gas money, and so what if I borrowed a little more. I'd give her my whole paycheck as soon as Uncle Rick saw fit to furnish me with one.

Someone tapped on my door. "Audrey?" Sara called.

Oh, so she decided she had time for me now? Whatever. "I'm busy."

"Can I—"

"No," I snipped back. "Maybe next time."

She didn't reply, and a minute later her footsteps moved away from the door. I didn't do anything that she hadn't done to me, but it didn't feel as good as I thought it would. We'd talk later. Maybe after a taste of rejection, she'd put aside her friends for ten seconds to hear me.

I shook my head to dismiss the interruption. Where was I? Oh yeah, the costume! The lady I commissioned Sailor Moon from also did props. I composed a quick email, added a few pictures, and sent it off. With a few more clicks, I ordered the rest of the costume pieces and materials. I could see it now. Kyle would probably open his mouth wide—half smile, half OMG—and then he'd run to me, drawing me tight in his arms. Heat rose up my neck and filled my face.

I forced my pulse to slow once again and took Mom's credit card from the desk. I'd pop it back into her purse late tonight, then I'd transfer in some money before it was due. No problem.

Every day for the next week, I'd find a package waiting by the door after school and rush up to my room, treasure in hand. Today's delivery was more special, because it had the belts and helmet I commissioned. More so, this was the last piece.

When school finally ended, I hurried home. I had to see what it looked like, what Kyle would see in a mere week. I slammed my car shut and ran to the door. *Whoa, what a huge box.* The lady must have secured the stuff so it wouldn't break, worth every penny. I held the glass door open with my elbow and dragged the box inside.

Inside my room, I kicked some scraps of fabric out of the way to clear space for the box. Newspapers covered the desk, where I'd finished cutting and molding the shoulder armor. The dyed Gi and costume pieces hung from the window valance, the closet door, and over the back of the computer chair. The energy pack was made of a painted cardboard tube, but it'd work. It looked like a Hobby Lobby threw up. I hadn't cleaned either, which left some wadded clothes strewn about. I'd have plenty of time to clean after the con, and after I saw Kyle.

I took my car keys and sliced open the tape. With the excitement that only comes Christmas morning, I rummaged through the pink Styrofoam peanuts and retrieved three packages wrapped in wads of newspaper. The two smaller ones contained the belts, but the large one had the helmet. I tore into the paper, and light from the hall touched my prize. The door swung all the way open.

"I'll help unpack the groceries in a minute. I've got to get this put—"

"What'cha got there?" Dan's voice hit me from behind, low and with a tone I couldn't decipher.

I turned to see him blocking the threshold of my room, in my house. He'd been in my room a zillion times, but right now, it felt strange. He shouldn't be here, not after he'd been avoiding me.

"Oh this?" With a final tug, I tore off the last layer of newspaper to reveal the detailed, faux-distressed, awesome finishing piece. "It's a Boushh bounty hunter helmet, the kind Leia wears when she rescues Han in *Return of the Jedi.*"

He whistled. "Nice. Must've put you back a pretty penny."

"Oh, the lady gave me a discount for being a repeat customer. Wasn't as bad as…you'd… What's the deal with the death glare?" I set the helmet on the carpet, pushing a few packing peanuts out of the way.

Dan let himself in, closing the door behind him. "Where exactly did you get the money for it and all this other stuff?" He flicked his hand toward the array of costume pieces littering the floor.

"Is that any of your business?" I stood and brushed the carpet fibers from my jeans.

He shook his head as he sighed the way parents do when their children act out for attention. "Sara's worried about you. Saw your package delivered last weekend after you stole your mom's credit card for gas money that same week. She wanted me to find out what was up with you."

I coughed. "What?"

"I'm concerned, too. What did it take to turn you into a thief?" His lips closed tight.

"I can't believe you. Not that it's any of your business, but I *borrowed* the money. I'll pay her back when your dad finally gives me a paycheck."

Dan's face tightened, like he was trying to hold something in, something explosive. He leaned over to grab the boot covers from the arm of the desk chair. "Yeah right. Did you 'borrow' anything from Dad's booth to finance your project here? Huh?"

"Oh my God. No, of course not. You're accusing me of stealing from Uncle Rick?"

"If the boot fits." He dropped the boot covers on the floor. Pink peanuts scattered, squeaking softly as they fell. "You stole from your mom, so what's my dad to you then?"

My jaw hurt from holding my mouth open so wide. "What the hell? I didn't steal anything. I can't believe you would even think I'd do something like that."

Dan's glare turned into a slow blink, his lips curving down. "I know you wouldn't. But, whatever assholes who did steal from us really screwed things up. Do you have any idea what that's done to us?" Dark circles under his eyes seemed deeper, and he wouldn't look at me.

I rubbed my forearm, making small ovals with my thumb. "What's going on?"

"A couple cons ago, some high-value items were stolen. Dad never found the cash we had either. On top of that, the city's trying to rezone the strip mall so they can tear it down for a Mega Mart gas station. Dad's been putting together a protest, getting support from the neighborhood and the other stores, but he's spent a lot of money." He ran his fingers through his curls. "He's taken out another loan to try and save the shop. We could lose the house."

"I had no idea…"

Dan snorted. "Maybe you should have asked."

"Who am I, Jean Grey? Am I supposed to read your frakkin' mind now?" Turning my back, I picked up the helmet and set it on the desk next to the armor.

"Guess that makes me Wolverine," he mumbled.

"Seriously? That's what this is, you're jealous." I bent and grabbed the boot covers by his feet. He didn't need to handle them so roughly, jerk.

"No." Dan huffed. "I'm worried 'cause you're acting weird. You'd never steal from your mom before, especially not to impress some guy."

I put the boot covers carefully on the chair. "That's not what this is. You don't get it."

He kicked a pile of Styrofoam; a couple pieces crunched under his sneaker. "Then tell me. What's so special about Boba Fett guy?"

"His name is Kyle."

"Whatever. He's a bad influence."

"No, you are." I yanked the door open, the sudden wind from the hallway ruffling the back of his hair.

Dan sighed. "Audrey, please. I really am worried."

"Shove it. And out. Now." I stood next to the door and pointed the way in case he forgot.

He crammed his hands in his pockets, hunching over as he turned. "Sorry." Then he disappeared around the corner. Footsteps announced his descent.

How dare he come into my room and accuse me of theft. That ass! I didn't deserve to be compared to whatever idiots stole from Uncle Rick. I just borrowed the cash.

A pit dug through my insides churning guilt like sour milk, or milk with orange juice added to it. Uncle Rick couldn't pay me. Apparently, he could barely make his mortgage even with Aunt Jill's part-time job. If she didn't have severe back issues, she could do more, but that wasn't gonna happen.

I glanced at my craft-store-disaster-area of a room, and my stomach churned harder. How could I spend money I didn't have to make a costume when they had real problems? I'd been so concerned with my needs, my worries, my appearance, my everything. Self-conscious or selfish, they were the same. I probably even got Kyle his car for my own benefit, so that I could see him again. And all he ever did was worry about other people. Had I ever done anything truly selfless? The knot inside twisted. No.

Waves of anxiety began to lap at my feet, slowly building those tiny invisible shakes through my legs, then arms and body. Great, now even my subconscious hated me for being stupid. As the tingles got stronger, I breathed in through my nose and closed my eyes. Giving into it now wouldn't help anyone. Making a plan, that's what I needed. How could I fix things?

Well, I couldn't un-buy all that stuff for the costume, but I could do something for someone else. I needed to help Uncle Rick's family. The store had been in trouble for awhile, and I should've done more to bring in business somehow. There were lots of advertising opportunities on message boards, social media, or local events, but they all cost money. That was one thing Uncle Rick didn't have.

The visor of the helmet caught my eye, so detailed it could've jumped right off the screen. The costume! I'd cosplay for someone other than myself. If I won a prize from the cosplay contest, I could donate it for the shop's advertising budget, maybe even plug the store when I accepted the award.

But to do that, I'd have to go on stage again. Could I? My breath began to quicken at the thought of walking out into the lights, to the audience, the stares, the judging…but no. I paused to focus and fought it down. I could conquer the panic for Uncle Rick's family. Doing the contest last time had scared me, because it was all about me. This was about *them*. To make it worth it, I really had to win. Dan had done tons of contests; he'd know how to make a run for first.

Dan, who I just shoved out of my room. Nice planning. Would he even hear me out if I came crawling to him for help?

13

Audrey

The high-pitched buzz of the alarm interrupted a dream involving some scary dudes on hover boards chasing me through an alley. If my heart wasn't speeding from the quickly fading weirdness, the noise had shocked it into overdrive for sure. I slammed the alarm off and dug my face into my pillow. Dumb clock. Didn't it realize I couldn't fall asleep until, damn, was it really just two hours?

The cause of the insomnia hurtled back into my head like a brick, with a headache to match. I had been so self-centered and hadn't even noticed. Dan, Uncle Rick, and Aunt Jill were on the edge of homelessness. And I forced Dan to listen to me whine about missing paychecks? What was I thinking? Though, he shouldn't have accused me of stealing. But…maybe he had a point about taking the credit card. Even before he told me about the thefts, the danger to the shop, and the loan, I didn't expect a check to come soon. Mom would get the bill long before I paid her back.

I lifted my face from the cotton refuge of my bed and sighed. Time to do the right thing. A confession now might get me grounded, but holding it back would be worse. My stomach flip-flopped, my head pounded, and my eyes hurt when I opened them. *Is this what a hangover is like?* And I didn't even get the fun of a party beforehand.

After throwing on some clothes, I ran a brush through my hair, and hurried downstairs to the kitchen. Mom was making ham sandwiches to the background music of the hissing Keurig. She assembly-lined three plastic lunch boxes with an assortment of fruit, trail mix, organic tea, and the main course. Her wavy hair was tucked up in a clip, and her striped blouse completed the teacher ensemble. She liked to wear professional stuff during tests, said it made the kids subconsciously more serious about it.

As she snapped the last lid, Dad flew by the line to grab one. He pecked her on the lips, then dashed away for his hour-long commute. Mom and I had a few more minutes to spare in the mornings. Minutes alone, like the confessor and her priest.

My early confidence regressed into head hanging and toe twisting, the hallmark of an embarrassed little girl.

"Here." Mom handed me one of the containers. "I put strawberries in yours."

"Thanks." I took the box and laid it on the marble island next to my backpack. "Um, can I talk to you?"

Mom turned, showing her best you-can-tell-me-anything smile. "Sure, honey. What's going on?"

How could I steal from *that?* My eyes watered, but I covered by reaching for the travel mug of coffee on the machine. I shook in a packet of Splenda and stirred. The usually comforting aroma nauseated me.

"Oh, thank you." Mom took the mug. "Are you okay?"

"Not really."

She frowned, trying to maintain eye contact, but I caught her click her phone so the date and time appeared.

Of course we didn't have much time; I'd just have to blurt it out. "I'm sorry. I know I should've asked, but I was afraid you'd say 'no' so I took it without permission."

"Wait, wait. What're you talking about?" Mom screwed the lid on her coffee mug.

I slipped my hand into my pocket. The card dug into the bends of my knuckles as I forced myself to pull it out. "I'm sorry. I needed the gas money. I got the costume stuff too, and I will pay you back. I planned on it, but Uncle Rick's paid me in merchandise for over a month."

Mom gaped. "You took my credit card from my purse?"

If I didn't feel like a godless hoodlum before now, that nailed it. "Yeah."

"You should've asked, Audrey."

"I know."

Glancing at the counter, her cheeks drooped and she looked way older than she should. "I think you need to readjust your priorities. If Rick isn't paying you anyway, you can stay home from the convention as a punishment. You won't be using gas or spending money, which it seems you don't have." She took her lunch and the credit card and zipped both into her insulated lunch pouch, pointedly looking away. "It'll be good for you to stay in the house longer than a few hours."

This weekend was AniSuperCon, and I had to enter the contest to try and win Uncle Rick some money. If I'd done more for them before, maybe they wouldn't be in this position. I needed to do *something* to help. And, Kyle would be there. I'd miss seeing him too?

The tears I'd succeeded in sucking in came flowing right on out. My breath caught short. I covered my face with the cuffs of my hoodie. Why couldn't I stop crying? I must look so stupid.

"Audrey, come on." She shook her head and slung her purse over her shoulder.

Her disbelief provoked the bawling reflex, devolving me from irrational crying into nonsensical hysteria. My throat started to hurt. I tried to stop it, but my brain had no control, as if I was watching the insanity unfold from outside my body.

Mom gasped. "I didn't mean to make you feel bad for having a job. I know I also spend too much time at the school. We'll make a family game night on a weekday or something, okay?" She dropped her bag on the counter, and her arms surrounded me like was still a child.

I buried my face into her shoulder, simultaneously wiping my eyes. "That's not it. I sound so dumb."

"What's wrong?"

Though Uncle Rick's failing store wasn't really my fault, Dan had been right when he said I was selfish. Giving them the contest prize would prove I could change, if only I had the chance. But Mom would think my idea was lame. Ugh, now I felt worse.

She repeated, "What's wrong, sweetheart?"

"But Kyle's going…" I couldn't explain the contest thing…and, I was desperate to see him. Who was I kidding? The thought of missing him was why it hurt when I breathed.

Mom nudged me away from her shoulder and lifted her brow. "Who's that?"

"I don't care if I skip any other con. I know I need to be grounded, but I…I…" My tears slowed enough for me maybe sound like my age again.

"Kyle's going to be there and he lives in Waco. I won't see him again for who knows how long, and I can't talk about it, but he's under a lot of stress and I…"

Mom's mouth slowly transformed from a half-frown to a little "O" of surprise. She blinked, her eyes sparkling like she was plucked directly from an anime. She let go of me, holding her hand mid-air. "*Kyle*, huh?"

"What?"

"Do you have a boyfriend?" She smiled, grinned, beamed, and every other word for happiness in existence.

Awkward parental romance involvement alert—level red! At that, my instinct to flee sucked my tears dry. I snatched my backpack. "Gonna be late. Gotta go."

She tapped my arm. "Wait, Audrey. We're not done talking about your punishment."

Fight or flight adrenaline charged me up, and all I wanted to do was run the hell away. "I'm sorry, I really, *really* am."

"And you'll show it by doing everyone's laundry for a month, mowing the lawn, and being in charge of the dishes. You'll prep dinner, clean afterward, and basically keep up the house without help."

"I can go?"

Mom smirked. "Working off the payment is more fitting. Besides, I don't want to put a cramp in your style." She covered her mouth, squeaking. "Oh, my little girl's first boyfriend."

My heart skipped, my stomach squirmed, and if I didn't escape, the authorities would find me on the kitchen floor dead from embarrassment. I nodded and hurried out the door, praying my blush would fade before I got to school.

After school, I pulled into the lot of the strip mall with Uncle Rick's store. Though the schedule didn't show Dan working today, his truck was parked in its usual spot. Weirder still, Uncle Rick was crouched outside by the window with a box at his feet and a big pile of wooden stakes on the curb. What was he doing?

I locked my car door and walked over. "Hey, slow day?" I bit my tongue right after. Why'd I say that?

Uncle Rick smiled anyway. "Yeah. But it'd be great if you could watch the store. I've gotta get these signs out."

"Signs?" Kneeling on the concrete, I opened the box and pulled the top one off the stack. In big red letters it said "Stop Mega Mart! Save your property values!" and had a website listed at the bottom. I cringed. "Did you make the website?"

He laughed his big cowboy laugh. "Dan made it."

"That's good."

As he struggled to balance all the stakes in his arms, a few fell and clattered on the sidewalk, one slipping off the curb onto the lot. Using my knees, I scooted over and picked up the strays. I maneuvered to my feet, and we dropped them in the bed of the truck. With an extra shove, the pile fell over into the back of the bed so the stakes wouldn't slide out once on the road. Dan should get the tailgate fixed, but yeah…money.

Uncle Rick heaved a sigh, wiping his forehead and then his beard. "I hope it's enough. If we can't get the neighborhood to make a big protest about this, then Mega Mart will convince the city to tear down this strip. I can't afford to relocate. I…" he shook his head and put on a smile. "Don't worry about it, hun. It's not something you need to fret about."

His smile stayed tight, but something in his eyes drooped and his shirt hung un-tucked, which wasn't his style at all. Had he looked this haggard before? Did I miss it?

"But I do worry." At least I did *now*.

"We'll do okay. I know the people in these houses don't want flood lights keeping 'em up at night. They'll make a big stink, and the city will keep the strip." He hefted the box into the truck next to the pile of wood.

"I can help put out signs, too. Maybe tweet the website."

Uncle Rick shook his head. "No. You help me tons watchin' the store while I'm out. You've done more to help us than I can say. I only wish I could pay you soon."

My help hadn't made any difference to their situation. No amount of cash register babysitting would pay his mortgage. "I'm working on a surprise for you."

"Yeah?" His fake smile brightened as crow's feet turned up.

I opened the door to the shop, bells tinkling. "Yeah. Just wait 'til AniSuperCon."

Uncle Rick's brief smile disappeared as he stepped onto the stirrup thing by the driver's side door. The promise of a surprise probably wasn't enough to lift the veil of gloom he was carrying around, but once I got that prize money, it'd stay away for good. I'd win it for him. I had to.

Kyle

Eric sat at a desk toward the center of the empty classroom, his pencil scratching furiously on the worksheet as the seconds ticked by. For his practice test, time probably went warp speed, but for me, the world stopped spinning. Everything moved so slowly that a day took a year, and the weekend was eons away.

I paced the perimeter of the room to give him space, which left me with nothing to do but wait. He'd finish the test, but I'd still be waiting for a whole week. Then I'd see Audrey at the con. The clock behind the teacher's desk ticked the end of another minute. Nine thousand eighty-three more to go.

My phone rang, and Eric's hunched form sprang open, scared like a ferret running from a knife-wielding bunny.

"You still have fifteen minutes, keep working." I grabbed the phone in my pocket, muffling the ringer with my palm. I glanced at the screen. Audrey? On my way out the door, I swiped to answer. "Hey."

"I didn't know when it was a good time to call." She sounded nervous.

I shook my head even though she couldn't see. "S'okay. Now's fine. Don't ever worry about callin' me." Hearing her voice beat reading a message by a hundred percent. No, a thousand percent. *Man, I really need a break from math.*

Audrey sighed a heavy breath, which crackled the speaker by my ear. "I want to do something to help Uncle Rick's business. I wanted it to be a surprise, but I need your help to have a chance of pulling this off."

"What surprise? Pulling what off?" I backed against the painted cement wall of the hallway, crunching the edge of a poster for the band boosters.

"I made a *Star Wars* costume. I'm not sure it's good enough for the six-oh-second, but I thought I'd try. I have two favors to ask. One, can you tell me who to contact about making really good armor? And there's an accessory piece that would look great made like the plastic on your costume instead of cardboard."

A *Star Wars* costume? It needed armor. Who would it be?

"Kyle?"

"Oh, yeah. Yeah, um…Josh helped me vacuform my Boba Fett stuff. I'll text you both. He's in Plano, so he's close enough to you to get it done this week." I paused. "What character?"

She didn't answer right away, and I could picture her biting her lower lip. A week away? Seriously?

"I wanted to surprise you, but I'm going as Leia," she said.

Wait, Leia, and she needed armor. The slave Leia bikini was armor, well, where it covered. Barely covered, and that cloth almost-skirt thing draped between her…the picture focused in my brain instantly. Wind sucked straight out of my lungs, like I fell backwards off a swing set, and heat rushed through my head so hot I would've registered a fever.

"Kyle?" Audrey asked.

I sipped in some air to reply. "Yeah, cool. Sounds awesome." The opposite wall of the hallway rematerialized, a ghostly shadow of Audrey wearing slave Leia clinging behind every blink.

"So, the other favor. Um, Uncle Rick's store is in real trouble. That thief at the con? He got away with some of their high value stuff, and now they don't have any money to spare."

"The security guard never caught up to him?" I asked.

"No."

The scene returned to my mind with all the shouts and commotion. I knew the guy had gone toward the hotel garage, because I'd heard a few voices that direction. If I had said something, maybe the guard would've arrested him.

Audrey broke into my thoughts. "I want to help with advertising costs to give the store a boost."

"What'cha need from me? Don't got a lot of extra cash."

"No, not money," she said. "Well kind of. I need to win the prize money from the masquerade contest. Will you enter it with me?"

"The contest? Me?" Acting in a skit? Remembering lines, public speaking...what part of that was a good idea?

She said, "I know it's not your thing, but I really want to enter. I'm not good enough on my own, but a skit together might be funny enough to win. Plus, your Boba is amazing."

"The con is only a week away." I tried not to sound desperate. Only? Way to change the relative definition of time with a switch in variables. That nailed it; algebra had killed my brain.

"Please?"

She was begging me to go on stage, when she planned to go up there wearing a glorified bathing suit? If she could put herself up there like that, I sure as heck could, too. Besides, the store only needed money because the thief got away. I should've stopped him, or said something to the security guard.

I kept silent then. I wouldn't make the same mistake now. "Okay. I'll do it."

"Thankyouthankyouthankyou!" Audrey squeaked. "We can practice Friday night when you get there and Saturday morning. I'll have it all set up. Don't worry about a thing."

"I won't. See ya then, 'kay?"

"Can't wait!"

The phone clicked off, and my body couldn't decide between excited and terrified. Both felt pretty much like I'd never sleep again. I had a week to build my resolve, a week to get ready, and a week before I got to see Audrey. And her costume.

Nine thousand seventy-five minutes to go.

Thanks to the miracle of math and my students catching on, tutoring let out a few minutes early and I made it home before Dad. I could fix dinner for both of us. But what if he ate at the office or got home really late? That'd be a waste of food. He'd probably want me to make a single and let him fend for himself.

I tossed a frozen burrito in the microwave, dutifully flipping it halfway through the cooking time, and brought it to a tray table in the living room. The quiet TV left the room feeling dead. I turned the TV on and flipped through channels as I took a bite from the center of the burrito. The ends masqueraded as landmines of molten cheese lava, and waiting five minutes allowed them to cool to the perfect temperature.

The door from the garage opened and closed, but I didn't hear the thud of Dad's briefcase hitting the floor. Yawning, Dad walked into the living room from the kitchen, his briefcase still in his hand. More work even after getting home so late?

He saw me, burrito half in my mouth, and nodded. "Oh, see you got dinner. That's good."

I choked down the bite. "Didn't know when you'd be back, so thought I shouldn't fix something big."

"I can get texts at work." He set down the case long enough to put up his coat and Marines cap in the closet, then grabbed the briefcase again.

"Oh…yeah. Sorry." The huge bite of tortilla and beans felt like it stuck in the bottom of my esophagus, a reminder my inconsiderate choice. Dad was overworked. I should've made dinner anyway or texted like he said.

Dad came over and patted my shoulder with his free hand. "It's all right. I'm not that hungry tonight." He gestured to my duffel on the floor by the sofa. "That reminds me. I got an email from the school about the JROTC summer program. They have an online sign up. Did you register?"

Oh no, he knew about it. Eight weeks of simulated army boot camp was the last thing I wanted to do. It overlapped with at least three cons within driving distance, too. Not only would I be pushed to exhaustion and yelled at daily, but I'd miss conventions where I'd see Audrey. No way.

I swallowed the chunk of food a second time. "Uh, no. I haven't."

"I'll get the registration started when I go upstairs then. I've got more work to do tonight anyway." He lifted the briefcase and gave me a smile.

"That's not nece…I mean. You don't have to."

Dad grinned the way he did whenever he came to a JROTC event. "It's no problem." He loved seeing me in uniform, but I loved the uniform I chose.

No way he'd get the hint, I had to say it. "No. I don't really wanna do boot camp this summer."

"What?" His grip on the briefcase tightened, making the skin of his knuckles stretch thin.

"It's so long, and I think the school year program is enough for college applications. During the summer, I want some…free time."

He exhaled slowly through his nose. "I see."

"Sorry, Dad. I know you want me to have the full experience—"

"Full experience? Dammit, Kyle—this is your life, not a spa brochure."

Sitting in the deep groove of the sofa, I felt trapped. I couldn't move. "But, I don't wanna go."

He dropped the case, and it fell sideways on the carpet. "Life isn't about what we want, Son. It's about what we need. You need discipline, structure, and character. You need to be a leader. You need boot camp."

I always did as he asked. I wanted him to be happy, to keep from depression, and I'd put myself aside. Why was he so dang intent on forcing me? "Well, *you* need my signature on the enrollment forms. You can't make me go."

He paused, picked up the briefcase, and looked at me. "Sure can't. Can't make you get on that school bus tomorrow morning, either."

School bus? But I had a parking permit, and…oh crap. "You can't…"

"Title is in my name. I could sell it if I *wanted*."

Blocked by the tray table and caught in the sofa, I'd never get out from under his shadow. It was my choice, my car or my summer. The car was the only way I'd get to see Audrey, which made the decision a fraction easier.

"Okay. I'll go."

Dad's quick smile reappeared. "You'll have fun. I promise."

I nodded and forced a smile in return. Dad went upstairs to the office, leaving me once again alone with my burrito and the chatter of the TV. I picked up the last chunk. The now-cold bean smell made me gag. I wasn't hungry anymore.

Audrey

The red light refused to change, holding me hostage at the intersection. Couldn't it tell I had to go? I needed to catch Dan at work. Every time I saw him at school, he'd find an excuse to flee the scene like I was radioactive and would melt his face off. Other kids were starting to gossip. That didn't bother me. His frown bothered me. If only I could hold him still long enough to explain my plan.

After ten thousand years, the light turned green and I zipped down the road, turned left, and swerved into the parking lot. Dan's truck was parked crooked in the spot on the corner. Thank goodness.

I went inside. The tinkling from the bells on the door stood in for the chirp of sitcom crickets. Dark even with the lights on, all the products lined the racks in immaculate rows. Why hadn't I noticed it before? Uncle Rick didn't mind making a mess at cons, because he'd have hours of "free time" to put it all away. The now-familiar sensation of guilt swam back into my insides, wreaking havoc with the remnants of my healthy lunch.

A light brushing came from the back of the store. Dan propped his head up with his elbow on the glass case by the register, leafing through what looked like the latest *Spiderman* comic. Must be a good issue; he hadn't noticed the door open.

Tiptoeing, I approached the counter. *Don't run away.*

He glanced up from the comic and straightened fast, putting distance between him and the case. "You, you're not scheduled today."

"If you bolt, I swear I'm going to lose it. I need to talk to you."

"We'd only make each other mad." Dan turned and went into the stockroom.

Damn it! That was how he always handled things, jerk. But I needed his help. I hurried around the counter and through the doorway.

Dan stood between shelves filled with boxes, clipboard in hand, and pretended to take inventory. "If you're gonna be here, you can watch the store."

"Come on. I'm sorry I threw you out, okay? Even though you should be the one apologizing for calling me a criminal." I snatched the clipboard away.

He gawked at his empty hand. "What the heck?"

"It's all for you guys, anyway. Listen to me for five seconds."

"Fine, I'm sorry. Give it back." He reached for the clipboard, but I held it over my shoulder out of range. He groaned, "All right, what is so frakkin' important?"

I exhaled and rested my back against the metal shelf. Uneven boxes poked my spine and shoulders. "The top awards for the AniSuperCon Masquerade Contest are cash prizes. First is a grand. I'm gonna enter, and I need your help with a skit that'll be good enough to win." I kept rambling, even though he was giving me a weird stare. "Then Uncle Rick can use the money for advertising. I can thank the store in my speech or something, which should help, too."

He blinked. "What costume?"

"My bounty hunter."

"Aud, you've seen the people who enter the contests. Big cons like that bring out the semi-pros. Your hack-job armor won't cut muster for craftsmanship, and the best skit in the world won't save you." Dan sighed, took the clipboard from my hand, and set it on the shelf. He opened and closed his mouth. "It's a nice thought, though."

Oh. My. God. Did he actually say that? The same friend who I subbed for with the Power Rangers sketch just said I couldn't compete? He'd forced me to go on stage, and now he couldn't be bothered to write a few jokes. Way to return a favor. I'd have a new prop by contest time, not that I'd bother explaining myself to him.

"Hack job?" My jaw popped.

He jostled a box as he leaned into the shelf. "Th…that…that's not what I meant. I'm just saying, you'd need to have a really detailed costume, and the presentation…" His lame attempt at an apology dissolved into mumbling as watched me glare. He stopped, took a breath, and forced his enthusiasm. "Maybe it can be amazing. What were you thinking of for the skit?"

I let my mouth relax and took a moment to calm down. He probably didn't mean to be a rude jerk, and I'd been poking the sleeping bear myself. We both needed to chill.

A hint of a smile came to his face. "Really. What was your idea?"

Now that he was willing to listen, everything I planned to say flew out of my head. He asked for a plan, and my plan had been to ask him. "I dunno. I thought Kyle and I could do some gag about losing a bounty, or really, I thought you'd think of something better."

His face discarded the tiny smile in return for rigid cheeks that sucked his lips into a black hole. He turned his head, shoving the clipboard back into an empty space on the shelf, and said, "I can't work with that." He moved along the shelf, trying to squish past me.

I pressed my shoulder against the boxes and blocked him. "Yes you can. You've got a million jokes rattling around in there."

"No. I don't." He pried my arm away.

"Come on, please." I pushed against him, trying to keep him cornered where he had to listen. He jabbed me in the ribcage. I flinched at the tickle, and he fled through the door.

Cheat!

I ran after and caught him behind the counter. I grabbed his arm. "I can't come up with something good enough. I need your help."

"Ask Kyle." He tugged his arm away, snatched his comic, and escaped into the body of the store. His back faced me while he returned the book to the shelf, and he remained against the wall to rearrange stuff that hadn't been touched all day. Would he ever be my friend again?

A pinprick jabbed my chest right over my heart. It hurt for real, actual physical pain. Watching him fake cleaning through the tidy store made each teensy jab stronger until the urge to cry robbed breath from my lungs. I held it back and rushed to the exit so he wouldn't see. I didn't want him to notice me at all, but those damn bells ruined everything.

I wiped my forehead, pressed the safety button, and squeezed the lawnmower handle. My shirt stuck to my back, stomach, and even my armpits like a second layer of skin. Gross, sweaty, dripping skin. I lurched forward like a minion of the undead, but I still had the whole backyard to go. Mowing the lawn in Texas should be a crime, or owning one, really. We should all have tasteful Zen gardens made of sand and rocks instead of yards of weekly torture. Dad gladly gave me this chore for a punishment, and that's exactly what it was. I deserved it.

I rocked the lawnmower back and shoved it over a tree root. It strained to cut the damp grass in the shade, sputtering almost to a stop. My sore hands released the lever; the engine cut off. I heaved and dabbed another liter of sweat from my face. Obviously, the chugging was lawnmower speak for "give me a break," and like a good lawn zombie, I complied.

Leaning against the magnolia's trunk, I waited for a breeze. Nothing. It'd take at least forty minutes to finish the back yard, and then I had to do the laundry, prep dinner, eat, do homework, and sleep. A similar schedule awaited me every day. When Josh had texted about the energy tank, I told him I'd never have time to meet up before Friday. Mom had been merciful to allow me to go to the con, but that's where her leniency ended. If I entered the contest with my "hack job" prop, I'd just embarrass myself. I'd never win that prize. Maybe I shouldn't go at all.

Kyle would be disappointed. I'd miss seeing him.

I miss seeing him now.

The thought zapped me awake with a longing pain. Real pain would dull it. I kicked the mower into life, and resumed a death march across Kentucky bluegrass. One more row and turn, push, push, push. Reach the end of the row, turn, and push some more.

The phone buzzed in my pocket, which was glued spectacularly to my leg. I stopped the mower and got it out to see a new message from Josh.

What's your address?

I wiped my hand on my shorts, three times, and tapped, *Why? I can't meet up. Grounded.*

Got some 602 guys to chip in materials. We made the energy tank for you. Drop it by tomorrow?

Josh and his friends made the prop for me? I didn't even ask. Despite the pain in my whole body, I smiled. *OMG I can't thank you enough.* I typed my address.

Great. Don't worry about it, Sailor Moon.

As I put the phone away, a half-sob lodged at the bottom of my throat. It didn't feel like crying, but the lump put a pressure in my chest the same way. I'd never experienced gratitude with such a visceral feeling. Kyle's cosplayer friends spent time and money on me, someone they didn't even know. Those elitist steampunk girls made me second-guess cosplaying, but I had no idea the wide differences that existed in the community—casual, pro, organized, solo, groups of friends, families, and people just trying to figure it out like me. Kyle's friends were probably some of the six-oh guys that do charity events, too. Better people could do awesome things. That's what I wanted to do.

At the last con, I posed with a little girl. She thought I was really her hero. Not quite the same as raising money for sick kids, but I had made her smile. One smile was a small start. I'd have to work harder.

The devil machine beckoned me, so I tightened my ponytail and started it up. Hard work wasn't in short supply.

Thursday night after dinner, I stood before my mother in the kitchen. Arms crossed and chin raised, Mom leaned against the counter as she looked me over. My warden waited a minute or two in silence. Long agonizing silence. If she didn't let me go out, I wouldn't have another opportunity to get the last thing we needed for the skit. It wouldn't make sense without a prop.

"Dishes?" Her gaze hit me straight on.

"Done."

"Lawn?"

I nodded.

"Laundry?"

"Whites and brights are folded and put away, darks in the dryer." I pointed to the laundry room, where the low hum of the dryer ran behind the closed door.

Mom sighed. "Homework?"

I had stayed up till two on Wednesday to finish the paper so I'd have time to run out. "Yup."

She cocked her brow to remind me I was still in trouble. I looked down, mouth closed and somber enough. After another slow minute, she exhaled. "Fine. You can run to the store, but you have to come right back."

"Thank you," I said, jumping forward for a hug.

Mom's wrath melted into a soft embrace, and she shook her head. "Hurry up and go before it's too late. Drive safe."

"Yes, Mom." I let go and grabbed my purse off the counter in the same movement. One more blink, the opposite of mom's interrogation timing, and I had gotten into my car, turned it on, and drove onto the road.

Thirty minutes later, I had survived traffic and arrived at the craft store. It was staring to sprinkle, misty drops of cold hitting my face and arms as I hurried through the parking lot to the glass doors. In full-on mission mode, I weaved between the displays toward the bargain section. The prop we needed was a little burlap sack I could sharpie some Aurebesh characters on that meant "Money." Unfortunately, the little bag would cost some real money. Hopefully the change I scavenged from my car and bottom of my purse would be enough.

I swore I saw something like it the last time I came. The bargain bins were filled with all kinds of random craft kits, toys, candy, and seasonally themed knickknacks. It took them forever to remove something, too, like they still had Halloween stuff out when the Valentines arrived. The money bag had to still be there. Where was it?

Almost to the end of the aisle and on the bottom row…pirate toys. I bent over to grab the burlap bag with the "$$" printed on one side (I'd turn it inside out for the skit), and a pair of strappy sandals appeared next to the bin.

Sara's shoes. What was she doing in the craft store?

Without saying anything, I took the pirate booty bag and straightened. "Oh sorry. Excuse me." I lowered my chin, avoiding eye contact so I could sneak around.

"Audrey." Sara's hand met my arm.

I flinched away, popping my head up. She looked back at me, her perfect lips twisted in a little knot as she chewed the inside of her cheek. I checked behind her, behind me, to the side, and found none of her worshipers around. Why was she here? She stood there like she was waiting for me to get with the program or to suddenly realize the grand plan.

The only thing I knew was that she'd been avoiding me, and I could beat her at her own game. I started to walk past her.

"Hey."

I should keep going, leave her behind. Ignore her just as she ignored me, but—always the but—the little voice that wanted her to acknowledge me shouted in my skull. How would she ever be my sister if I didn't let her?

"Why are you here?" I turned around.

Her shoulders dropped. "Can we talk?"

"Sounds like it."

She did that weird chewing thing with her lips again. "Listen, I'm not good at admitting I'm wrong."

"Newsflash."

"Seriously, Aud, let me apologize!" Sara's exasperated grunt ended in a squeak, like her voice got all tight in her throat for a second.

Maybe this *was* real. I thought back, but couldn't remember her ever saying sorry unless prompted by Mom or Dad. Here she was, downturned eyes as she fidgeted with the strap of her purse. Was it possible she meant it?

I took a step back to open space between us. The sprinkle outside began to pelt big raindrops against the windows, and they made hollow-sounding pings on the roof. "Okay. I'm listening."

"I'm sorry I told Dan about the credit card. I didn't know he'd go all psycho on you about it." She slid her hand down the purse strap again. "I was just worried. Mom said you came clean, and I don't know, I felt bad for butting in when I should've known you'd do the right thing."

Sara's words swam past me in a river of nonsensical sound. The stolen credit card? What about dumping me at the costume store to hang out with her friends? What about ignoring me? What about her complete ignorance of anything in my life—cosplay, Kyle, my stupid idea to give myself a panic attack on stage for Uncle Rick's sake. "You don't even know you're doing it, do you."

"What?" She cocked her head.

"You dumped me for your friends you've known two seconds, even after all that shit in middle school. Hell, you ignored me at home. You're ashamed I'm your sister." Once I started, everything exploded like soda from a can someone shook for a prank. "I'm sorry I don't cheer, or dance, or wear winged eyeliner. I'm sorry I'm not popular."

Sara's hand stopped fidgeting, she stopped chewing, and her mouth slacked open into quivering lips. "I don't...I," she sucked in a breath, "I don't think that at all."

"Sure as hell don't act like it." And as I said it, a shimmer coated her eyes and she pressed her fingers to the corners to keep tears from coming. Tears...real tears.

My hands started to shake and my stomach dropped.

She sniffed and blinked wide, dabbing her eyes until she stopped the impending doom to her mascara. "You're right. I didn't notice." She paused. "I'm sorry."

"Really?"

"Yeah." She took a step, like she was gonna hug me, but stopped herself.

Gripping the burlap baggie in one hand and my purse in the other, I closed the space to finish the hug for her. "I'm sorry, too. Can we start over and ignore the last few months?"

"I'd like that." She squeezed me once and let go.

I smiled. "I'm glad I let you talk." Wait, she'd had to track me down to talk to me at the store, when she could've easily waited until I got home. "How'd you know I was here?"

"I told Mom to call me when you came to town."

"What? Why?"

Sara fidgeted with her purse again. "If I tried to catch you at home, you'd brush me off again. I needed an ambush."

"Ahh..."

She looked at the doors, which were now streaked with rain. "So, um, hey. I know. Let's get a couple double caramel lattes, my treat."

The caffeinated sugar olive branch sounded amazing, and what made it better was that she offered first. "I'd love that."

She walked to the end of the aisle toward the registers, and I followed. The *tings* of raindrops echoing throughout the store like music.

"I don't mind the rain." I gripped the costume prop. "But, Mom said I had to come—"

"It's fine." She put her arm around my shoulders, and as we approached the checkout line, she opened her purse. "Don't worry. I got this."

The cashier rung us up right when Sara's phone began its barrage of *dings* once again. Her friends, of course. Guess I'd be kissing that coffee goodbye, along with the bonding. At least I got a half-baked apology and a free prop out of the deal.

Sara swiped her card to pay and checked the phone. Her other arm squeezed my shoulder as she lifted the phone above us, her head pressed next to mine. "Smile." She snapped the selfie and sent it off as a reply message, which she held for me to read.

Sorry, girls. Sister time today. Laterz! :-D

My jaw unclenched, feeling strange and loose after holding in all my annoyance. "You sure?"

"Absolutely."

My body still felt tense and a little shaky. After all, Sara taking time for me was strange after all the days she chose someone or something else instead. Part of me didn't believe her even now, when we were walking out together in the rain to get in her car. Trust would take time to rebuild.

Sara buckled, shifted into drive, and gave me a little smile. I smiled back. Trust went both ways, and I had just as much work to do.

16

Kyle

The last few paragraphs of my essay took every ounce of brainpower left. I skimmed through the opening and sent the file to print. Done, finally done. The printer began to warm up, which meant rattling loud enough that the neighbors probably wished I did my homework earlier in the day. Downstairs a noise shook the floor enough that I felt it through the clatter of the temperamental machine. It was the door closing. Dad must be home late again.

I hadn't seen him much the past week. Some days I'd nearly be in bed, and he'd come in to say good night. Other days he let me go to sleep without a word. He probably didn't know I stayed up late to finish the paper. Maybe I should check up on him. Lack of sleep and overtime had to be taking a toll, which could lead him in a downward spiral again. Keeping on top of things was key.

I left my room and heard the baritone of his voice. He was talking to someone? I crouched at the top of the stairs.

Dad talked into his cell, his tall body bent from exhaustion. He cracked his shoulders as he sighed. "No, no. I'm glad we got the case. Mega Mart will pay premium to make sure they get that land, and having two cases means double."

Pacing, he nodded along to the silent half of the conversation. "Yeah. I'll do the digging for you. Off record of course. Yes." He paused. "Does this mean I'll get comp time?"

Why would dad want extra days off? He didn't even use the days he had, always working weekends, nights, all the time.

His briefcase hit the floor with a smack. I flinched back behind the wall. Did he see me? His voice got softer, so I poked my head around the corner.

Dad deflated into the recliner as if he couldn't hold his weight. During the day, he'd storm around with authority, throwing himself into work one hundred percent, and maybe that kept him going strong. Momentum.

"No, you can ask. I just…" He closed his eyes. "I have that open mic town hall soon. The real problem is the council's approval rating has gone down, but I can't get through to him. He's been acting up ever since that convention thing. I don't know what to do. He wasn't like this before."

Like what? How was I supposed to be? I hadn't changed…at least, I didn't think so.

The pitch of Dad's voice went down. "Thanks. I'll try." He hung up and let his hand fall to his side, phone in his palm. Worn creases took hold of his face, and his frown deepened. It hurt to look at.

Sneaking off to the convention last time had hurt him. It must've been that I lied about it, but what choice did I have? He wouldn't let me go, and the six-oh was the only thing *I* actually choose. Band, JROTC, even tutoring, they were all Dad's ideas, his plans for me, his interests. I had to keep something *mine*.

No matter what, I was going to AniSuperCon to see Audrey. I promised her, and broken promises left wounds. I wouldn't be the one to do that to her. Dad couldn't know about the trip, and with the cover I came up with, he wouldn't. Another lie though.

Dad's eyes closed, his chest rising and falling with deep breaths, but that frown was stuck deep in his cheeks. My stomach clenched. No, I wouldn't hurt him, because he'd never find out. I'd be there for him *and* Audrey.

Stale sweat odor hung like a noxious cloud inside the gym. I waited in line with the rest of the Waco JROTC with my feet shoulder width apart and hands clasped behind my back. In a stifling uniform surrounded by twenty-five teenage bodies, the act of resting was absent from the long stint in "parade rest." To my left, Garrett made weird faces, sticking out his tongue and rolling his eyes whenever Sergeant Macke turned his back. Garrett's lips puckered into a fish face.

I snickered quietly.

Sergeant Macke spun, his face inches from mine. "Something funny, Porter?"

Not quiet enough.

"No, Sir." I leveled my chin, eyes forward.

"Tell the rest of us what made you laugh, Porter." Sergeant Macke kept his nose right in front of my eyes, trying to make me blink.

I pried my lids open wide. "Sweat tickled my neck, Sir. Sorry, Sir."

He'd tried to intimidate me, but he never had a chance. A little chastising or push-ups only meant some extra sweat. As soon as I could get my butt in my car, I'd be an hour and a half from seeing Audrey. The Friday of AniSuperCon had finally arrived, and even Sergeant Macke couldn't keep me away from her. Heck, getting on stage for the contest tomorrow seemed doable as long as I could see her.

"If I catch you goofing off again, Porter, you'll be on the track until I'm tired of watching you run." Macke straightened.

"Yes, Sir."

The sergeant pivoted and marched down the line to finish his speech. At long last, he said, "Dismissed."

Oh, thank the Maker I didn't have to stay late. Now, onto Project Alibi. Everyone scattered to get their belongings. I dashed to the chairs along the wall, grabbed my duffle, and followed Garrett to his locker.

He hadn't noticed me as he spun the lock and jiggled it open.

"Hey, got a minute?" I stood to the side, behind the gray metal door.

"What's up?"

I waited until he closed the locker. "Told my dad there's a JROTC retreat this weekend."

Garrett blinked. "You what?"

"I'm going to Dallas. Cover for me?"

He balked. "You can't expect me to call your house or something."

"No, no. Just if he calls you. You're the only friend whose number he has. Please?"

"Fine. But you'll owe me."

I laughed. "After you just got me in Macke's crosshairs? I think we're even. Thanks, Garrett."

Instead of waiting for Garrett to protest or call it off, I dashed around the corner to change in the restroom. I didn't need to haul the uniform with me, so I tossed it in my locker and jogged out to the parking lot.

After being inside all day, the piercing day star hurt my eyes, and I shielded them with my left hand as I slowed to a walk. I grabbed my phone, and squinting, sent a quick message to Audrey.

OMW see you soon.

I stopped and then added, *<3*.

The trunk opened with a click. I tossed my backpack next to the box containing my Boba Fett costume and travel necessities. After the last con, Josh shipped the stuff I had left in the room. Forget the JROTC, there was nothing like the family connection within the six-oh, and Josh had even helped Audrey with her Leia costume. Damn…he got to see it before me. Of course, she probably didn't wear it for him. My ears burned, and I shut the trunk.

Like right before a classic alien invasion, a shadow blocked the glare from the sun. What the—?

"Don't you have JROTC right now?" Dad's unmistakable voice rumbled from beside his truck, which was parked next to my car.

Oh no. No. Not now.

I breathed deep, like Sargent Macke taught me, and kept my voice even. "Yeah, I'm fixing to head back in. Was gonna go to the retreat with Garrett."

"You're not in uniform." He crossed his arms over his huge chest, and backlit by the sun, I could barely see his face.

The lie wrestled with my stomach. He didn't know. He wouldn't. "We…uh…we're not, I mean, we don't have to 'til we get to the camp."

He didn't reply right away. He stood there, watching, and I wished I could see better. Dang sun.

"Open the trunk." Dad stepped to the side, and the new light revealed his expression—flat. His mouth locked tight, his whole face without motion, except for the glimmer of something in his eyes.

Day-long heat had cooked the asphalt into fumes, which got stronger every second. Fighting the urge to throw up, I rolled my shoulders and anchored my boots to the parking lot. I'd already committed to the story. No turning back. "Gonna be late, and I don't want Garrett to have to run laps 'cuz I kept him."

Dad's jaw cracked. "How many lies you gonna to spout to my face, Kyle?"

"Dad…"

"I know that damn costume is in there. Open the trunk!" He pounded his fist against the trunk, and it made a loud pop as it un-dented.

Panic tore through me like a tidal wave. I couldn't back down. I had to go. If I missed Audrey now, I might as well call it quits. She needed me in the contest to help her uncle. She'd sounded desperate, and I *wanted* to go. I wanted something for me. I'd given up so much to make him happy, to build him up, everything. I deserved to go.

"What's the big deal? It's just a con. None of the people voting for you are even gonna be there." I put my hand back in my pocket, balling the keys in my fist.

"My reasons ain't your business. You lied to me. You keep lyin' to me. I didn't raise you to disrespect me like that." His accent got stronger whenever he lost his temper, like he'd lost control. "Gimmie the keys."

The keys dug into my palm. "No."

Dad sounded calm. "All right then. But you drive out of here, and it'll be the last time." He took out his phone and turned it on. The screen showed my car, the sale price (way too low for the mileage), and a big green button that read "Sell." He put his finger a centimeter from the screen.

The car was my only freedom, but if I didn't see Audrey at the con, she'd give up on me. Hell, I'd give up on me. "Wait!" I pulled the keys from my pocket.

He stared, holding his finger over the button.

I handed him the wad of keys and keychains. "Don't sell it."

"Get in the truck. We're goin' home." He returned the phone to his pocket, but at least he hadn't listed the car. If I lost it, I'd never get to a convention again, or even up to Dallas. He might have gotten the keys now, but I wasn't giving up. I promised Audrey I'd see her. I had to find a way.

Audrey

Thick gloves made handing out change difficult. I counted one, two, three fifty-two into my palm and carefully transferred the cash to the latest customer. My Leia bounty hunter looked better than I'd hoped. The hard-plastic energy pack was practically a real prop. I almost scared Josh with how I jumped in erratic circles when he came by to drop it off. He hadn't asked for payment or anything. I'd have to make it up to him and the others somehow, since the energy tank really made the costume. Other attendees seemed to think so, too, which brought more interest to the booth.

Uncle Rick had balked when I suggested wearing the costume while working, but after the first guy who asked for a picture walked away with a bag of goodies, he was sold. He stood beside me, ringing up customers and rearranging merchandise. While he counted money, I counted hours. Long, long hours. When was Kyle gonna get there? We'd need to practice tonight as much as we could.

A bearded fanboy held a handful of old comics in my face, er, my helmet's face. "How much for all these?" he asked.

They were a set from the dollar comics, a few newer Marvel titles on top. I thumbed through the stack. "There's twenty-seven, so twenty-seven plus tax."

He cocked his brow. Oh right. I adjusted my helmet onto my forehead like a pair of sunglasses. "Did you get this one, too?" I lifted the newest Batman issue that he had in his stack, which didn't jive with the rest of his choices.

"Yeah, Bats is the only DC I read."

"Have you seen the pin set from this series? They took some artwork directly from the latest story arcs." I bent down, trying balance the helmet on my head, then I felt a nudge in my side.

Uncle Rick handed me the set so I could show the customer.

"Oh, awesome. I'll take that, too." The customer grinned, another happy adventurer successful in his quest.

I rang him up with an extra twenty dollars to add to the day's earnings. Upselling trended way out of my comfort zone, but somehow, I knew Leia would have no problem talking to people. Check that in the win column for the cosplay-dealer combo.

Something poked me on the shoulder. Uncle Rick smiled at me, so I plucked the helmet all the way off my head. Hairs escaped from my braid stuck to my forehead.

He said, "Thanks. I know you don't like doing that."

"I wanted to help." I hadn't been doing enough before. Hopefully tomorrow night, I'd win the prize that'd put simple upselling to shame. I had a ton of ideas for promotions. We just needed the funds.

"Thank ya, hun. You do so much for me. I'm so sorry I haven't paid you properly. If we can run Mega Mart out of the area and keep the store, I'll take your whole family out to dinner." Uncle Rick's graying beard looked dull even in the horrible ballroom lighting, but beneath it, his warm smile lit him up.

He didn't deserve to have his petty cash or those valuables stolen. He didn't deserve to have his life-long dream of running a business fail. Kindhearted men like him should have all the success in the world, but that usually left them trampled by the mean ones. For once, the little guy, or in this case "the old guy," was gonna come out on top. Kyle and I would win that contest.

That was, if he ever showed.

An hour later, Kyle still hadn't shown. Business increased as more attendees arrived at the con scene, and I sold a slew of add-on merchandise whenever I could. The good sales weren't enough of a distraction. Every passing minute where Kyle didn't approach the table inched forward slower than the autograph lines. Eventually the dealers' room closed. Still no Kyle.

My phone hadn't buzzed, dinged, or beeped since his *on my way* text, which he sent over four hours ago. It didn't take that long to get there. What if he got into an accident? Was he okay?

With my hand still in my belt pouch, I emerged from the ballroom into a crowded convention hall, bursting with Friday night excitement. A gaggle of girls in spiky wigs rushed me, cameras and phones cocked and ready.

"Can I take a picture?"

"Oh wow, that's an amazing costume!"

They mobbed me right off, and I wasn't even wearing the helmet. The braid had gotten tangled, and my face probably looked sweaty and gross. They wanted pictures of that?

A girl held up her phone and snapped one. "Dude, exactly like the one in the movie."

I heard a different girl's voice from behind, a familiar voice. "Good paint job, too."

She walked into my line of sight with her other steampunk superhero friends, the girls who mocked my Sailor Moon costume before. Here? A couple of X-Men were mingling with them, the same duo that won runner up in the first cosplay contest I entered with Dan. Those guys must be elitists, too. Great.

They meandered between me and the next two people wanting pictures. Without my blessing, my heart rate spiked, and I breathed slowly.

"Hey." Miss Steampunk America waved at me, all smiles now. She didn't recognize me at all. "Did you make it yourself?"

I pieced some together, bought some, and the six-oh guys made part of it, but what did that matter? Cosplay was about fun, not who spent the most or who hand-stitched a million yards of an embroidered gown.

The green girl made a scrunched-up face. "My friend is talking to you. She asked about your costume."

Though I could hardly breathe and my body wanted to run and hide, I stood still. I swallowed. "Could you please move. She's trying to take a picture."

Steampunk chick balked, like how dare I defy her epicness, then she scoffed loudly. "Come on, let's get to that leatherwork panel." Her friends followed after, allowing the photographer to get a shot of me.

I did it. I spoke up, and the world didn't end. The nerves of anxiety calmed into a quiet hum of power I had no idea existed. No panic attack, no tears, and if I could do that, I could take the stage tomorrow night, too.

I posed again with a smile of victory. If only Kyle was here to see.

More people rushed forward, and a semi-circle of photographers and fans formed. When one person left the line, another took the empty slot creating a bow of never-ending flashes. I smiled, posed, and fit back into my role. I paid attention to the younger fans who took photos with wide-eyed excitement. I gave them those smiles. But underneath the fervor of debuting my costume, an uneasy current penetrated my skin. Every camera flash lacked a companion at my side, and worried thoughts distracted me from the fun I should be having. Was Kyle okay? What happened?

Why didn't he come?

After a while, the crowd dispersed, freeing me to wander the con floor. I kinda wanted to go to opening ceremonies, but the squirmy feeling through my body pushed me away. I found myself at the elevator bank ready to return to the room. It was late anyhow. Talking to strangers and trying to sell bonuses all evening had worn me down.

I drifted through the hall and to the hotel room. Inside, Uncle Rick was sitting on one of the beds watching the TV broadcast of opening ceremonies. Dan wasn't back yet. He probably had more to do, which saved me from a boatload of uncomfortable exchanges.

Uncle Rick pressed a few keys on his laptop, to tally the sales for the day, no doubt. "Hey, hun, back for the night already?"

That'd been the plan, but Dan could come back at any time. He'd sleep on the cot and I'd have the bed, like we'd done at a dozen cons before, but now? How could I wear pajamas in front of him? How could I act like nothing had changed?

"Nawh, I'm heading back out. I just want to get outta this costume."

Uncle Rick nodded and returned to half-watching, half-working. I hopped into the bathroom to change out of Leia and into my *Infinity Games & Comics* T-shirt. If I didn't plan on sleeping, I'd at least advertise as a walking billboard.

I wandered around the main floor for awhile until I found an empty spot down the video room hall. The script for the skit crinkled in my pocket. I took it out and sat cross legged in the corner. Since I wrote the jokes, I already knew my lines, but Kyle's name stood out on the paper. Could I do it alone? I'd have to do a walk-on. That wouldn't be enough to win. The skit was the only saving grace; I needed him.

An uncomfortable tremor glided over me. Too much time had passed. What if something awful happened to Kyle? Worst-case scenarios seeped past the fake walls I had erected, and instead of thinking about stage fright, my brain blessed me with car wrecks, or domestic violence, or sudden illness that landed him in the hospital. Those were all so unlikely, so irrational, but a persistent voice in my head said *what if* enough to make my stomach cramp.

Breathe in, out, focus. Let it go.

My head hit the wall behind me as I released a sigh, eyelids closing. I blinked them open and checked my phone—midnight. No wonder I was dead on my feet. I allowed my eyes to close, and right as I was about to fall asleep, my phone chirped.

My heart leapt, then pounded. I fumbled the stupid thing out of my pocket. A message from Kyle. He was okay. Thank God.

Here finally. Where are you?

My fingers wouldn't cooperate. Auto-correct couldn't save my inability to type. Voodie? What was wrong with me? Ugh. I walked down the hall, tying to send a message at the same time.

Another text popped up. *I'm outside ballroom.*

Jogging turned into a full run. There, out in the main hall, Kyle waited by the doors sans costume. It was really him, fuzzy head and all, and he grinned as soon as he saw me running.

I glomped him with a leaping hug attack like a fangirl on her favorite voice actor. Kyle fell backward, taking me with him to the floor.

He yelped, then laughed. I giggled, squeezing him tighter around his shoulders.

The worry I had buried swelled forward, and my breath caught. "You're okay. When you didn't show, I thought something had happened."

His skin blushed all the way from his neck and over his head, obvious under the sheared hair. I was laying on top of him—full contact.

I scrambled off, heart thundering and my own skin flushing in an impressive red. What was wrong with me? How did I just *do* that! I covered my nose and mouth with my hands to prevent myself from hyperventilating. Just like in a paper bag, in, out, in and out.

"Hey," he said.

"Hi." I took a breath, hoping my face had cooled some. "I was just glad to see you're okay."

He stood and reached to help me up. "Sorry I didn't text. The phone was dead 'til I charged it in the car, and then I didn't wanna text on the road."

"What took you so long?" I grabbed his hand, and after I got to my feet, I didn't let go. Neither did he.

"Dad figured out I lied about where I was going. He took my keys. Lucky he put 'em where he stashed my phone last time. I had to wait 'til he fell asleep before I could sneak out, then walk all the way to school to get my car."

I squeezed his hand to steady myself against the firecrackers exploding all around and inside my body. He did all that for me? To come see *me*? "You really snuck out. Walked to school? I…wow."

"Made a promise, didn't I?" He smiled, his arm scooping me to his side. "Do I wait 'til later to admit I'm terrified of going on stage, or is that not manly or something?"

"You're not alone. I've only done it once before, and it was under duress. I hate the spotlight. I hate the stage, and I'm freaked about doing it at all," I said.

He squeezed my waist. "Then why're we doing this again?"

"Because Uncle Rick is super nice, and he deserves some help. It's the best thing I could think of."

"He's lucky he's got someone like you." Kyle swallowed. "Know I am."

The swoon factor tripled, and for some reason, practicing was the last thing I wanted to do. But, we had very few chances…damn. "Nice one liner. Ready to learn a few more?"

Kyle nodded, and we walked hand-in-hand through the hall to an empty corner.

I handed him a folded packet of papers. No one else had read my skit. It might suck. Would he think it was funny? I watched his eyes flick back and forth as he read the dialogue, and his brows crunched inward.

"Is it that bad?" I asked.

He scratched his head. "No, no…it's good, but I'm confused. Didn't you say you were doing Leia?"

"Yeah, the Boushh bounty hunter. We'll match!"

His face rounded, mouth open. "Ooohhhhhhh. Armor. I see." When the realization faded, his mouth slacked almost in a frown.

I wrung my fingers together and looked away.

Kyle grabbed my twisting hands. "That's a hard costume. Never woulda guessed you'd try to make something like that, and just so you could match mine?"

Gunk formed in my throat, and I swallowed it down. "I don't know if it's good enough for the six-oh, but I wanted to try."

He didn't say anything right away, and when I looked up, he gave me an awkward smile. He released my hands and wrapped his arms around my back, hugging me tight. "You never fail to surprise me. Can't wait to see it."

Kyle

Bubbles of something ephemeral floated me in space as I curled to the side. On my shoulder, the soft world purred. It tickled, rumbled, and snorted?

My eyes opened. Rows of empty chairs filled the room up to the movie screen at the front. After practicing our lines until we couldn't think, we had crashed in one of the video rooms. From the weird angle, the flickering images could've been anything, and for a moment I pictured a giant spider or a fifty foot woman. Someday, I'd watch those cheesy drive-in movies with her.

Audrey startled as she straightened off of my arm, where she'd fallen asleep. My shoulder ached and my back throbbed from sleeping crouched in the chair, but it felt spectacular. She was right here next to me. A bent spine and a few bruises were the best gifts in the universe.

"What time is it?" Audrey yawned and rubbed her eyes with her knuckles.

I pressed my phone. "Four forty-five."

She snickered. "Early start to the day, huh."

"Or late night." I reached behind her shoulders, replacing my arm where it belonged.

She relaxed into my side. Warmth swaddled my body, and for once my heart calmed instead of speeding. It felt natural and normal, and love filled me with the same comfort as hot coffee in an ice storm. That's what it was—love. Being with Audrey swept away all the worries about Dad, about anything but us. Not that I'd say it out loud; that'd be idiotic.

"Since we're both awake, want to practice a couple more times before I have to work?" she asked.

Did I want to? No. Would I? "Sure. We don't wanna look dumb on stage."

She grabbed my hand. "The dead-pan delivery sounds so funny. I think we can win. Don't you?"

"Got as good a chance as anyone else." I stood, stretching some of the ache from my numb shoulder.

We shuffled out of the row of seats and to the corner of the hallway where we practiced before. Audrey took her position on the opposite wall. We counted, then walked to the center as if it were the stage. She brightened with her animated smile, exaggerating every motion like a living cartoon, as I recited lines and tried to remember my cues.

She grabbed the script from the floor and let me read it again. "Almost, but I think we missed a line."

Something glinted in the light, moving behind us. A tall figure blocked the hallway toward the artists' alley. No, impossible.

Dad formed an unbreakable barricade that demanded attention. I thought he'd follow me, but so soon? Before I left, I'd made a choice to do something for me. I deserved to have a choice.

"Come on." I squeezed Audrey's hand, tugging her forward.

She gasped.

Dad lurched to the side to block us. "Tell your friend goodbye. We're goin' home."

I met his gaze. "I promised I'd do the contest for her. I'll be home Sunday."

"Promised?" His eyes widened, and he opened his mouth without sound as if I'd struck him. "What do your promises mean, anyway? You lied again. You came here."

Audrey's hand kept hold of mine, but it didn't stop the squirm inside that echoed Dad's words. *Liar! Selfish! He'll spiral again, you'll see. Months of darkness will be your fault.*

"I...I..." Another hand squeeze.

"Tell your friend goodbye. We're goin' home," he said again.

"This is insane. How'd you even find me?"

Audrey stood close. She even put herself slightly in front.

Dad held out his phone, swiping it off the lock screen. A map appeared with a little green dot blinking our location. "Why'd you think I didn't bother taking your phone?"

"You tracked me? I can't believe you'd do that." I threw my hands in the air. "Come on, Dad, aren't you taking this too far? It's just a convention. Not sacrificing small animals behind the library or dealing drugs."

"If you could see yourself just now, acting like a child, you'd understand. The internet is forever, Son. Playing dress-up won't get you a partnership at a firm." The phone shook in his hand, and his thickened accent sounded unsteady. "I work like a dog for you, pay for your food, the house, your uniforms, retreats, everything. I've taken care of you for six years. Ever since…"

Dad caught his breath and straightened. "And this is how you repay me?"

"Dad…it's just a…" But my mind blanked. He was right. Dad had worked his ass off for me, and I ignored what he needed.

Audrey let go and stepped forward, her black T-shirt acting like a narrow shield. "He'll be home Sunday."

Dad eyed her for a full minute, and I swore I saw a smirk. What was that about? "I don't need both sets of keys. I'll list your car for sale. Don't make me." He reached out his hand like a peace offering made of anything but peace. "Let's go home?"

"You don't have to." Audrey's lips pouted, and even without the glitz, they made my heart ache.

I had to go.

When Mom died, Dad was so lost. It'd been the two of us for so long, and when I drove to the con, I made a choice all right—I forced him to worry alone. How could I leave him like that? He'd suffered enough. It was my job to protect him from ever going down that road again.

Between feeling like a slug for abandoning my dad and possibly losing my car, I'd be a mess well before it came time to get on stage. Audrey would probably never want to see me again after this. The warmth in my heart from earlier hardened into a deep ache. I just couldn't win.

"I'm sorry." I took Dad's hand and turned away.

"Kyle…" She said my name, not with shock, but with a half-broken squeak. The sound burrowed down my ears, rooting into me to make sure I'd know I hurt her. Dad, Audrey, me…we all lost. I formulated a problem with no solvable answer, which set us all up for failure.

Dad pulled my hand, and I walked down the hall, Audrey behind me. I wouldn't look. She'd shown me a million expressions—anime grins, fierce stares, roaring laughter, and a loving smile. Whatever face she wore now, I didn't want to see.

As soon as we cleared the hallway, I let go of Dad's hand and walked behind him, watching my feet. Sneakers marched over ugly carpet, polished tile, and onto the stained floor of the garage elevator. We waited quietly for the doors to close. I'd gotten used to the way he shouted without saying a word as my mind fill in the blanks.

A selfish, horrible excuse for a son. Who would abandon and lie to his widower father? Me, that's who.

The only thing Dad had muttered before then was a promise to send a colleague to get my car on Monday and that I had to ride back with him. And at the same time, I imagined Audrey left back there in the wake of my broken promise. She couldn't help her uncle now, and it was my fault. When things went wrong, it was usually my fault.

With a shake and a bump, the elevator opened to the parking garage. I looked up. The packed lot made it hard to see my car on the other side of the divider—that I deserved to leave behind this time—but Dad's truck was parked in a spot up close.

Dad palmed his keys from his pocket, making the truck beep and flash its headlights as it unlocked. "When we get home, you're still grounded, but I'm glad you made the right choice. I didn't want you to force me to do things y'all would regret later."

"You mean sell my car?"

He walked to the driver's side of the truck and paused. "If you keep up this bad habit, I might still have to. It'd be worse if your actions affected that girl, wouldn't it? So, let's forget this mess and get back to normal."

The already-unreal world froze as I replayed his words in my head. *It'd be worse if your actions affected that girl.* Wait, no, he couldn't have. Did he threaten Audrey? The dim lighting of the parking garage darkened into tunnel vision, closing in like the absence of light had a mass, a weight that could crush me.

"What about her?"

Dad slid into his seat and reached across to open the passenger door. It swung wide in front of me, lengthening the tunnel to an endpoint. "That store on her staff T-shirt, *Infinity Games & Comics*, is listed as an obstacle for one of my client's cases. I'm assuming she cares about the place, and the case could go either way up there in Dallas."

Watching through the truck door, Dad seemed as if he'd ordered a burger and fries, that nothing insane and horrible had spewed from his mouth. Unfazed and businesslike. Was that how he handled his cases in court? The small, dark tunnel around me squeezed into nothing, and I stood in a void of what-the-hell.

Did Dad even care that I broke a promise with her just to ease his mind? Did he realize I effectively lost a girlfriend for the sake of making it up to him and sparing his feelings? *His feelings?* Did he actually have any, or was his depression an act to get me to play along? Did he even care? How could someone who loved me even think about ruining someone's life to force me to "step in line?"

I sucked in a breath against the pressure of the contracting world between us. "I can't believe you. That your philosophy at work too? Do any awful thing you need to win?"

"I only want you to understand the severity of your actions, and that it's important to listen." He sighed, shaking his head. "Get in. It's late."

Revulsion crawled over my skin, and I couldn't look him in the face anymore. He'd play games with a case to hurt Audrey and her uncle, only so I'd do what he wanted. I couldn't. No way.

"No." I grabbed the truck door and slammed it shut.

"Kyle!" Dad yelled. "What the hell are you doing?"

Dad's little mini-me voice in my head ticked away. *He'll spiral. Your fault. Once you get home, it'll suck. He'll hate you.*

But those words were lies. They were always lies. Maybe six years ago, the eggshells had mattered, but things had twisted into something insane. What he was doing was crazy, and I didn't have to listen to it.

No more.

I silenced the voice and pivoted on my heel to march with purpose, as JROTC drilled into me, back to the sliding glass doors of the hotel entrance. The truck slammed closed again, followed by Dad's hefty footsteps.

He grabbed my shoulder, but I tore it away. "Get back in the truck," he ordered.

Lifting my chin, I looked him straight in the eye. "I can't sit next to you right now. I'm going to the con. I'm doing the contest, *for* Audrey, and maybe when the weekend is over, I might be able to stand talking to you."

"How dare—"

"No! How dare *you*. You'd ruin some guy's business just to get at me? What the hell?" I walked to the doors, which swooshed open and blew cold air onto my skin.

"Watch your mouth."

Ignoring him, I continued my march into the hotel tunnel toward the elevator. Dad's shadow stayed over me.

He huffed, deepening his drawl. "Fine. Just remember, this is for your own good."

The elevator dinged, doors opening, and I walked inside, trying to appear like my world wasn't dissolving or that my insides weren't disintegrating into puddles of goo. As the door slid closed, Dad's form stormed off, shaking the floor in his wake like an earthquake.

19

Audrey

Alone, sitting in the empty hallway, I scratched through another line on the script. And another. Damn it. The skit wouldn't work as a monologue at all, and there's no way I could win best craftsmanship as a walk on. I'd failed Uncle Rick, wasted the money I spent on the costume, and felt like an absolute loser. Do a duo costume with Kyle? That'd be great…if he had cared to stay.

I slumped against the wall as every ounce of energy seeped out like a slow leak in a tire. Pressure had built so strong when I was worried about Kyle, but if he couldn't see how his dad treated him, how could I do anything to stop it? He willingly left. He'd be okay, wouldn't he? Without the motivation that I could help, I emptied. He had given up, so I could give up too.

My head thumped against the hollow breakout wall, and I stared at the ceiling. As I crumpled the paper into a ball, hurried footsteps pounded down the hall. Kyle ran, then slowed to a walk, breathing hard.

Everything felt slippery, like an anime dream sequence where you don't know what's happening. How was he here? Kyle couldn't have left and be here at the same time. It simply didn't make sense.

But he *was* there, standing in his wrinkled shirt and jeans, the same clothes he wore while we snoozed in the video room. A little funky smell of sweat, too. Maybe he was real.

Kyle held open palms of surrender. "Sorry. I'm so sorry. I shouldn'ta left."

I opened my mouth, but nothing came out. I looked away.

"I know. I promised I'd do the skit with you. I came back, and I'm so sorry." He paused. "Just felt bad for abandoning my dad, too. It's a sucky situation, because after my mom—"

"You know what, that does suck. But so does your dad." I snapped my head to look Kyle in the face. "I'm sorry your mom died. It's horrible. But your dad is using that as an excuse to control your life, and it's not normal. It's not good."

His brows wrinkled in, and he gave a little shake with his head that he probably didn't realize. "Grief changes people. I know. He can't help it, and I'm only trying to do my best for everyone."

"Everyone but *you*!" I stood, balling the crumpled skit in my fist. "What's your dad going to do when you go to college—register you for classes he wants and make you commute from home?"

He shoved his hands in his pockets. "I know. I know it's bad. Didn't realize how bad before, and I'm trying now. S'why I left him and came back here. He…" He looked at the floor. "I really like you."

"That why you left me? Uncle Rick needs that prize money."

"Audrey…I'm sorry." Kyle's shoulders rolled down, and he didn't say anything else. He seemed lost in thought.

My balled fist shook, the crumpled paper poking my palm. Didn't I mean more to him? How could he just leave me like that?

A little bump twitched between Kyle's eyebrows, and though he was staring at the carpet, I could see his face scrunch and squirm. My irritation let go, allowing my sore heart to swell. He was probably hurting and confused, and if I held a grudge, it'd only make things worse. Maybe I could get through.

I released my fist, and the ball of paper hung loose in my fingertips. "It's not your fault either. I just want…you should be happy."

"I'm trying. Promise I won't give into him like that again." He paused like he was thinking. "What's really goin' on with your uncle's store?"

The papers felt heavy in my hand, so I backed up to the wall to find something solid to lean on. "He needs money since the shop isn't doing great, and he spent a lot fighting this zoning thing. He took out a loan."

"Zoning thing? That something that involves the court?" Kyle's voice sounded higher, weird. What was wrong?

I nodded. "Mega Mart wants the land his shopping strip is on."

"Oh…oh." He returned to that odd look he had before.

"What's going on?"

He popped his head up like he was startled. "Oh, nothing. Thought I heard that name before."

"You probably have." I watched his face for an explanation, but he said nothing. Something strange was going on. Kyle would tell me eventually, wouldn't he?

The awkward silence hung there like an uninvited guest. I didn't want to be mad at him anymore, and he *did* leave his dad to come help me. He cared about me, too. We could get through it, especially when we rocked it in the contest.

"I've got to work in the dealers' room today, but we have time to practice now." I added, "If you want to."

Kyle nodded fast, too fast. "Yes. Yes I do."

We took our places on our pretend stage in the hallway and practiced all morning until it was nearing time for the dealers' room to open. As it got busier, we relocated to a corner, though people kept interrupting to walk in and out of nearby rooms. I knew my lines by heart, and Kyle got into his role so well that I had to keep from laughing. Part of me laughed anyway. The other part kept nagging about when Kyle had left. I thought he'd be gone for good, but it had only been ten minutes until he came running back. His dad must have said something worse than usual. What had he said? Why was Kyle acting so cagey?

To my left, Kyle slipped his phone into his pocket. "Almost time for you to work." He smiled, but something seemed off.

"Yeah. I…um, we can meet here at five in costume and have a bit to roam before lineup time." Though I smiled, the voice in my head repeated my worries.

He nodded, tapping his hands on his legs. "Okay."

In the pause of goodbye, I should hug him or kiss him, and I wanted to. I couldn't. Something unsaid ballooned an invisible force field between us, which made me ache all over. I waved my fingers and kept a smile on for him as I trotted away. Someday, he'd let his shield fall and allow me close to him. He would.

I hurried to the hotel and back to my room. Not only would I need to work in costume, but I wouldn't have time to change afterward. I went inside. The light was on.

Uncle Rick's voice came from around the corner. "Dan, did you find her?"

Oh no. I hadn't checked in at all last night. "Hey, Uncle Rick."

"Audrey!" He appeared at the foot of the bed, relief obvious in his tired eyes. "What happened? Why didn't you answer your phone or come back. I have the hotel staff out looking for you."

"I'm sorry. I turned off my ringer in the video room and forgot to turn it on again." I hadn't even thought about Uncle Rick getting worried. I'd been so concerned about Kyle that he completely fell off my radar. "I'm sorry," I said again, like it could somehow erase my carelessness. After I swore to think of others instead of myself, I failed my first test. Why was it so hard to get out of my own stupid head?

He swept me into a hug with shaking hairy arms. "I'm just glad you're okay. Where were you all night?"

I patted him on the back as my stomach inverted in on itself. "Just roaming the con. I passed out in the video room." Which was true. I wouldn't mention practicing for the contest. I wanted that to be a surprise. After I gave him the check and an awesome marketing plan, he'd be so happy that he'd forget about my mistake. I'd make up for this and a thousand other times I ignored the issues with the store.

"Next time call, okay?" He let me go and sat on the edge of the unmade bed, which groaned under his weight. His body looked soft and round, like his muscles had released their hold after hours of strain. He'd been really worried.

"I swear. I'll be heading to work in a few minutes, just need to get the costume on. That okay again?"

Uncle Rick's wrinkled brow finally straightened as he chuckled. "More than okay. I want you cosplaying every convention. We made it into the black for the weekend yesterday alone, thanks to you."

"I'll do my best." I saluted.

"See you at the booth. I'm heading down."

"Sure thing," I replied and went into the bathroom to change.

With Uncle Rick's blessing, I finished my shift and fought through the swarm to get out of the dealers' room. Being in costume all day turned my bounty hunter armor into a Dune-esque stillsuit, where I could collect my sweat to repurpose it for life on a desert planet. Unfortunately, or fortunately really, I didn't live in a desert, and so my sweat went from precious resource to nuisance. I didn't have time to freshen up. Kyle was waiting for me. I hurried past the crowd in artists' alley and toward the video rooms.

The hours working allowed me to ignore the weirdness from earlier. Kyle was standing up for himself now. He came back for me. Warmth fluttered inside, sending a blush to my cheeks. Thank Lucas for helmets with masks.

Boba Fett sat cross legged next to the door to the first video room, head hung like he was sleeping. We had essentially stayed up all night, then his dad went psycho on him, which had to make him more tired. Poor thing.

I knelt by Kyle's side and tapped his shoulder. He jerked up, helmet turning every which way. He stopped when he found me and took it off.

"Audrey? You…whoa, really?" He grinned and covered his ever-changing expression. "I can't believe you did this yourself. It's awesome. You're awesome."

The mask hid my deepening blush. "I'm glad you like it."

"You're right, and the judges are gonna love it." He ran his hand over his buzz cut. "Not as much as I do, though."

The word *love* stuck out as if he paused ever so slightly beforehand. Maybe I imagined it, but he seemed to emit some kind of light, like a glow-in-the-dark toy that had been buried in the bottom of a box for years to finally find the energy it needed.

I offered my hand and helped him up. "Let's get a photo op in before the contest."

Kyle smiled, which looked normal now, and popped his helmet back on. "As you wish."

We walked out into the fray. It only took about ten seconds before the amateur photographers noticed us, and we got stuck in a spot along the back wall for the next thirty minutes. Kyle posed with me in coordinating shots. Flashes, laughter, bizarre photobombs, and everything—just like I dreamed. I could do it for hours, if we had hours or if I hadn't been on my feet in costume since before dawn. The stuffy helmet began to make me dizzy.

I waved off one photographer. "I'm sorry. We need a break."

Kyle took my hint and helped extract us from the group, back into the crowd, but as soon as we were free, another person tapped my shoulder asking for a picture. I shook my head and they left. The Sailor Moon costume hadn't been this popular. I could get away without being constantly mobbed.

"Follow me," Kyle said. "I know where to go 'til lineup time."

At the end of the gaming hall, a handwritten sign reading "Cosplay Corner: No pictures" stuck to a small breakout room. Kyle and I ducked inside, closing the door behind us. A single table against the wall provided a few complementary bottles of water and a bowl of Doritos. Folding chairs were scattered throughout the room, most of which were occupied.

A guy wearing a home-sculpted foam velociraptor costume collapsed against the right-hand wall. He pulled off his dinosaur head, sweat beading all over his red face. A girl sat by the table, her iridescent gown poofing a foot on either side of her, and her feather headdress cascaded down her back into a train. One of the other cosplayers wore a Tron-inspired jumpsuit, wired with LEDs and light-up tape. Oh my stars and garters, we had to compete against them? Dan was right. We didn't have a chance.

I found a pair of chairs and claimed one as I began to visualize all the ways we could fail on stage. Why'd I think of this stupid plan? We would go make idiots of ourselves for no reason, no prize, no check, no advertising. It'd be a waste of the inner layer of my stomach lining from all the extra stress.

Kyle sat next to me and put his hand on my shoulder, what he could reach of it anyway. "Take off the helmet and get some air."

"I'm fine." If I took it off, Kyle would see how freaked I was. He finally sounded comfortable with the skit, and we couldn't both lose control. Maybe he could forge confidence for me this time.

He wiped his glove over his face to soak up his sweat. "Come on. Only got a little bit 'til lineup for the masquerade. We need this chance to relax."

Of course he was right. I took off the helmet and the rapturous breeze from the vent swept over my face, forehead, and neck. Cool and magnificent. I'd barely been able to breathe in that thing. I set it by the chair and basked in the glory of oxygen.

"Better now?" Kyle asked.

"Yeah, you were right. We needed a break." Now that I could breathe, my throat gummed up. Those bottles of water beckoned me like a mint-condition issue to a fanboy with money to burn. I could already imagine the thirst-quenching relief. "I'll get us a couple of bottles."

I pried my tired butt off the chair and over to the table. I uncapped a bottle and drank so fast that water ran out the corners of my mouth and down my neck. Sweet, cold, glorious water.

"Excuse me?"

Gulping a last swallow, I tilted my head to see the guy next to me. He was wearing a Magneto costume, sans helmet, but the molded armor attached to his magnificent cape looked extraordinary. Real metal rivets reflected the overhead lights like mirrors. Wasn't he hanging with the steampunk girls?

"Are you talking to me?" I asked.

"Yeah, do you have a minute? I could use a hand." He held out a roll of duct tape and nodded toward the door. "My friend's costume came loose, and I can't hold it together and tape by myself. Can you help for a sec?"

I glanced at Kyle, whose head lolled to the side. I should let him rest.

"Will it take long? I have to get ready for the contest," I replied.

He nodded fast. "Yeah, us too. It'll just take a sec."

Though I saw him with the elitists earlier, he seemed kind of normal, nice even. Kyle said before that most cosplayers were good people. Maybe this guy didn't know how crappy his friends could be. If he needed help, I'd help. We were all in this together.

I followed Magneto out of the Cosplay Corner and down the gaming hallway. Inside one of the rooms, a crowd had gathered around a table of miniatures, but the others seemed less popular. Most were empty late on Saturday when the good panels took place.

Dude led me to the end of the hall, but it didn't curve around the corner like I thought it did. It was a dead end. Where was his friend?

Crack!

My chest slammed into the wall. Something tugged on my costume, dragging me back, but then another loud *crack* hit my back again. I screeched, covering my head with my arms. I could see a hammer in the guy's hand, and a second pair of legs.

One asshole grabbed a hold of my bandolier by my shoulder and yanked. It pulled me with it, and I yelled, "Stop! Help!" I swung at his legs, hitting him in the back of the knee.

He stumbled and another tug ripped my sleeve at the shoulder. I reached up, but he kicked my wrist, sending a sting all the way into my elbow.

"Stop!" I yelled again, cradling my wrist.

The other one stepped into view, the Apocalypse guy. He hit my armor with the hammer, and he tore off a chunk.

I ducked to the side, trying to get around him. The first jerk blocked me, lunged forward, and tore my sleeve down the arm.

"Get away from her!" Kyle's voice boomed through the hall.

They turned from me and ran toward Kyle, one squeezing by on either side of him. Kyle just about flew when he changed direction and went after them.

I'd follow, but my legs refused to work. I was shaking, no…I was crying. Without my costume, I was nothing. No help to Uncle Rick, no match for Kyle, and no freedom. I sat on my knees and heard my shattered energy tank crunch beneath me, and at that moment, my heart made the same noise.

20

Kyle

The assholes who hurt Audrey barreled past me, but to hell if I was gonna let them get away. I chased them down the hall, gaining easily. JROTC's obsession with fitness had its perks. The short gaming hallway opened into the main convention space outside the dealers' room and main programming. Damn, it was packed tight, bodies wall to wall, and all of them undulating about each other to go a thousand directions at once.

Magneto ducked left, and Apocalypse thrust straight into the mass of bodies, swallowed by the blob. I tailed number one around the edge of the room.

Someone bumped me from the side, and I stumbled into the wall.

"Excuse me," she said and kept on going.

I looked up, and of course—gone.

Damn it! Those jerks attacked Audrey, and I couldn't even scream in their faces. What was I planning to do anyway? Whatever, it didn't matter. I failed to protect her. From the first time I met her, I promised to be her bodyguard. I swore to keep her safe.

Another broken promise.

The anger inside had no outlet. It just charged through me, tensing my shoulders, arms, hands, and curling my fingers into fists. I kicked the wall. Cement. Ouch.

Damn it!

I leaned into the wall and pressed my forehead against the deep textured wallpaper, or whatever it was. The grooves dug into my skin as blood drained from my face. My stomach turned, and all the angry energy released its hold.

What had I done? I tore off after those jerks because I was pissed, but I left Audrey alone when she needed me. I left her again...*idiot.*

A vice squeezed inside, making me sicker. I had to get over it and go find her. Ignoring the awful pain in my gut, I hurried back the way I came.

At the end of the gaming hallway, Audrey was sitting on the floor. I ran faster, and as I got close, I slowed to a walk. Thin black trails curved from her eyes around the contours of her cheeks, glistening with her tears. Her beautiful lips puckered while she sniffled at the end of a wave of crying. How could someone *do* that to her?

I knelt by her side and put my hand on her knee. "Sorry. I never shoulda nodded off like that. I shoulda kept you safe." My chin dipped to my neck. "I'm so, so sorry."

She sucked in another breath, more tears cascading down the worn trails. It looked like she wanted to talk, but she couldn't. She leaned forward to put her head against me. I wrapped my arms around her. Feeling her tremble drove my self-hatred to a new level.

"Were you hurt badly?" I asked.

Audrey shook her head.

"I swear, for real, I won't let someone hurt you like this again. I don't know how, but I have—"

"It was my fault for trusting that guy. He said he needed help." She lifted away, wiping her eyes with the fingers of her gloves.

I sighed. "I'm glad you wanna help people. That's good. You're good. They're the ones who suck."

Her hands quivered in her lap. She clasped one over the other; they didn't stop shaking. "I was supposed to be stronger. I was supposed to be like her, but I'm not."

"Audrey..."

She ducked her head and pulled off the plastic part of her costume. She cradled the molded chest and neck guard in her lap. The prop energy canister was shattered, and bits broke off the armor, too. The jerks had even ripped a chunk out of her sleeve, so it exposed her upper arm.

Audrey looked up. "I was going to use the prize money to help Uncle Rick's store. The city wants to tear down the shopping strip to build a Mega Mart, and he took out a loan, and they can't make their mortgage, and Dan hates me, and I stole money from my mom to make this damn thing, and I can't even do anything—"

"Whoa, whoa, slow down. I know you wanna help your family, but their financial problems are not your responsibility. You don't have to feel like it is." I scooted closer and put my arm around her, which was easier to do without the broken costume bits jabbing me.

"I know." She sniffled. "But I did take my mom's credit card. I screwed up, and I thought if I used this costume to help the comic shop, that it'd even things out. I know it's dumb. I just…I really wanted to win this for them."

Audrey was taking their troubles onto her shoulders, when I was the one who could've actually done something about it. The store only needed money because I couldn't say two words to that security guard back then, and later I abandoned her to go with my dad, which was stupid. I'd failed her too many times. I wouldn't let her give up now. "Who says we can't?"

She blinked, water pooling over her eyes. "What?"

I stood and lifted her broken armor to examine the damage. "Looks a little bit like you scarcely survived a battle. The judges don't know that wasn't our plan."

Like a magical girl transformation, her expression slowly morphed from devastation to hope. She reached around and crushed me with her hug.

"Thank you," she whispered.

I didn't know what to say. I couldn't form words, anyhow. My arms found their home around her, and I rested my head next to hers. Everything was gonna work out okay.

From my belt pouch, I slid my phone into my lap and texted Josh and Mike, our garrison leader. Maybe I couldn't find the jerks who hurt Audrey, but I wasn't alone.

The masquerade contest was a headline event, which meant it took place in the giant ballroom next to the dealers' room. A stage filled most of the front area with floor-to-ceiling curtains hanging on either side.

The hour waiting backstage before the contest flew by, and the next thing I knew, the emcee had announced our names over the speakers.

I tried to draw slow, deep breaths through my nose. Whatever the audience thought of me didn't matter, and if Dad was embarrassed, that was his problem. I had to do this for Audrey. Across the stage in the other wing, I could only see her helmet. Was she scared? Was she worried? The helmet nodded, and she gave a thumbs up.

An invisible force jumped from her simple gesture, across the stage, and to my body, laying an unreal calm around me. Her bravery took me up the steps to meet her on stage.

I put the microphone next to my helmet's speaker. "What the heck happened to you? Have a party in a garbage compactor?"

She yanked off her helmet and shook her head, holding it in the crook of her arm like a boss. Her messy hair looked just like Leia's, which only made the costume better. "Some of us actually get into real battles." She rolled her eyes, tossing her head to exaggerate for the audience.

"I survived being eaten by a sarlacc without damaging my highly profitable and iconic ensemble. Plus, it makes me look totally badass."

The crowd laughed at my line, right on cue. The skit was working! We played off the enthusiasm of the audience. Audrey dove right into her cosplay role—all big smiles and over-the-top gestures. Of course everyone loved watching her perform. I always did.

At the end, I caught the judges chuckling to each other and scratching something on their notepads. Audrey clasped my hand, we took a bow, then we retreated into the wings. We didn't stop until we got to the hallway again, past the back of the line.

My helmet hit the floor with a thud, and I grabbed Audrey the waist, picking her up in a spin. "Holy crap, we did it!"

Her laugh echoed like the ring of victory bells. "You were great."

The judges wouldn't announce the awards for another hour, but that didn't matter. We already won, because we had gotten through it. I'd never wanted to go on stage or compete, but if every time made me feel this euphoria, then I'd do it again, and again!

Audrey squished me in another electrifying hug. Our armor smacked together, and I could hardly reach around her.

"Thank you," she said.

I let go so I could see her face. "No, I should thank *you*." Because of her, I stood up to Dad, I tried something new, and I enjoyed it. I'd never felt this kind of rush before…only a little because of the contest. Most of it was Audrey. "I'm…Can't even think of what to say."

She grinned. "I totally get that."

Kyle

Still encompassed by *holy-crap-I-actually-survived-a-contest* jitters, we sat against the wall with the rest of the contestants waiting backstage. When the time for the awards ceremony arrived, a few con staffers in black shirts guided all the exhausted cosplayers behind the curtains. We crammed into each other on both sides of the stage, feathered wings and prop weapons jabbing people left and right.

Audrey gripped my hand, and though we were both wearing gloves, I could feel her touch. The pressure of her fingers squeezed my knuckles, our palms pressed flat. She glanced at me. Something had changed. Oh right…for her, the contest only mattered if we won the prize for her uncle. Her strengthening grip mirrored her nerves, and dang she was nervous.

"We did great," I whispered. "We got this."

She replied with a half-nod and a bottom lip chewed within skin-layers of bleeding.

I pressed my thumb to her lip, freeing it from potential harm. "Breathe."

A faint smile appeared. My heart stopped.

"Okay, everybody." The emcee's voice blasted over crackling speakers. "Who's ready for the awards?"

Audrey's crushing hold resumed cutting off blood to my fingers. As long as we placed in the top three, she'd have a good chunk of change. I squeezed her hand, too, but doubted she could feel it as tense as she was.

"First award will be the Tailor's Award for best craftsmanship." The applause died down, and the emcee pulled a name out of an envelope. "Laurie Mills as Empress Firebird."

The girl wearing the elaborate ball gown and feather headdress pranced up the stairs and onto the stage. She bowed, claimed an envelope, and stood to the side onstage.

"Next, we have the judges' award for funniest skit." A pause as he pulled out the name. "Goku Times Nine Thousand!"

I exhaled in relief as the group of six guys in various Super Sayian Goku variations took to the stage. Each spiky, blonde wig rushed by in a blur. We didn't get that prize, so it meant we had a chance.

My fingers started to throb.

The emcee drew out the ceremony for all it was worth. He brandished another envelope. "Now, onto the overall set. Honorable mention goes to Bounty Hunter Duo!"

Bounty Hunter Duo…that was us. I snapped my head to the side. Audrey had plastered on a smile, but I could see the disappointment weighing all around her. We took our bows and accepted the twenty-five dollar Hobby Lobby gift card before standing in the line of winners. We *were* winners, to me, to the judges, but not to Audrey. As soon as she could, she put her helmet on. She probably wanted to get off the stage.

The names called after us muffled into background noise, that was, until they announced the grand prize winner.

"Apocalypse and Magneto, come to the stage. Show off those awesome costumes one last time." The speakers boomed and a strange ringing replaced the sound. My heart pounded, blood whooshing through my ears. No, it couldn't be them.

It was. The same jerks who assaulted Audrey rushed onto the stage. They stood six feet in front of us, smiling as they received their prize from the judges, bowing in their faultless, unbroken costumes.

My fingers curled into a fist.

"Ow." Audrey tugged her fingers in my grip.

"Sorry," I whispered, releasing my hold.

She turned toward me. I couldn't see her face through the mask. Was she going to say something? Right now, up here in front of all these people? Maybe I should speak out. They didn't deserve to win after what they did.

I lifted my boot to step forward, but Audrey squeezed my arm.

She shook her helmet *no* then leaned in next to me. "This isn't the way to deal with it. I don't think we lost because of the damage, and attention is what they want."

"But—"

"Thank you for wanting to."

The drumming in my ears didn't stop, nor did the shake in my blood that made me want to get them. But she was right. We had to lead by example and show what real cosplay meant, that being a good loser was just as important, or more important, than winning.

The asshole champions took their bows, and after the rest of us joined for a curtain call, we were released to escape the stage. Never letting go, I pulled Audrey away from the mass exodus. I kept Magneto and Apocalypse in my periphery. They stood in the open convention hall, surrounded by a handful of plain-clothed kids and the steampunk girls, who had also been bitches to Audrey. Made sense that assholes would flock together.

Audrey removed her helmet, shaking sweat from her hair. She handed it to me. "I'll be right back."

"Wait." My voice came from the speaker. I didn't want to drop her prop. "I'm your bodyguard, remember? I'll give 'em the riot act for ya."

"No. Not Aran, not Boba, not Leia, no other persona. I need to do this. Me." Her pink lips squished into a firm line, eyes dry and fierce.

"I'll wait here."

Audrey marched toward the pair and their meager group. She lifted her chin, pointing an accusing finger at both of them. I couldn't hear what she said over the chatter, which got louder as more people exited the ballroom. It got more crowded with each second.

I maneuvered through the exiting flow to get closer.

"Cosplay isn't life or death. It's a freakin' contest. You could've hurt me." Audrey kept her tone surprisingly calm.

"Like you said, it's just a costume." Apocalypse jerkwad had the gall to smirk.

Her mouth gaped, and she looked at his friends. "He came at me with a hammer!"

Magneto's helmet hid most of his stupid face. "How're you gonna prove it?"

After Audrey's disgust passed, she reached into her belt pouch. "I'm calling security."

With a lunge, Magneto swiped the phone from her grip. He held it high in the air. She jumped, but one of his friends nudged her with his shoulder. She lost her balance, falling to the floor.

That was the wrong move.

I ran a few steps. Two of their entourage blocked me, like football-style defensive line shit. Dad had me watch more than enough games to know the trick to a good offense. I shoved the one guy in the chest.

"Whoa, dude. Back off," he said.

"Audrey," I yelled over his head.

My phone vibrated in my belt pouch. Probably Dad trying to guilt me into going home. I didn't have time for that now.

In a crack between the two guys, I saw Audrey get to her feet and cross her arms in front of her chest. She wasn't backing down. Neither would I.

Clop, clop, clop.

A swarm of white, red, and gray double-stepped it from the tunnel entrance into the convention hall—mostly stormtroopers and clone troopers. Groups of people dispersed around the lines of armored cosplayers like oil dropped on water. They circled the jerks, though Audrey was caught in the middle as well.

On a hunch, I checked my phone.

JoshVader: Found them. Cosplay contest wasn't a good place to hide.

Smiling beneath my helmet, I stowed the phone and took my place among my brothers, right behind Audrey. There we stood, two sides of the same fandom.

Our garrison leader Mike, in his high-ranking stormtrooper armor, stepped into the circle to address the dark side. "One of our members witnessed you assault this young lady. He'll swear to it as well. Someone is fetching security, but if you try to make a run for it..." He gestured to the impenetrable wall of plastic armor.

Apocalypse and Magneto seemed a loss for words. Their friends snuck past the line of stormtroopers, and the elitist girls swarmed away from the drama as if they didn't know the guys in trouble.

"Hey, come back here!" Apocalypse ran a few steps, only to be blocked by the troopers linked arm in arm.

Magneto cursed. "I'm not paying the room bill."

The pair spent the next few minutes flinging curses in the direction their former friends fled. Security arrived and escorted them from the convention.

Audrey and I gave our statements, and once they left, most of the other attendees had either gone to their hotel rooms or found parties to crash. With the ups and downs of the past few hours, crashing sounded pretty good. Sleep, not partying.

We found a quiet corner next to a potted palm. Stray con-goers passed through the hall next to us, but we were otherwise alone. Audrey didn't say anything; her unfocused gaze stared at the far wall.

A million thoughts ran through my head, how she was brave, stunning, beautiful, and any other synonym for magnificent that existed. "You were amazing," I said. *Really? That's the best I could do?*

Her head jerked toward me. "Oh. Yeah? I dunno. I couldn't really do anything. If your friends hadn't shown up…"

"I woulda."

She smiled momentarily, and that dazed look returned. A movement near her waist caught my eye. She'd pulled out the gift card prize we won, holding it with her fingertips on the corners.

"Want me to go with you to your hotel room? I don't feel comfortable leaving you alone."

Audrey fidgeted with the gift card. She flipped it over and back again. "Nawh. Uncle Rick and Dan are in the room, and I don't think I can face seeing either of them tonight." She paused. "Would you mind crashing in the con suite? I know it's technically for volunteers, but I don't think they'd notice. Then I wouldn't have to talk to them 'til tomorrow."

"Sounds fine to me."

She texted someone, probably her uncle, and then we left the dark corner to head to the hotel. Soon we arrived at the con suite, a double-wide room on the top floor where convention staff kept a twenty-four-hour supply of food. Well, food-ish. Boiled hot dogs and a slow cooker of chili resided on the bar by the sink, and a tray of sandwiches lay on the narrow table behind the sofa. Three staffers manned the room. One at the table snacked on a family-sized bag of chips, and two more had passed out on a sofa and loveseat. The suite had two exits, the door we came in and another on the far end of the same wall.

Audrey tugged my arm. We sat by the TV and leaned against each other for support. She snuggled into the crook of my arm as if her body fit the precise contours mine created. In less than a minute, light snoring came from her allergy-infested nose.

I smiled and tucked my other arm around her. An internal buzz always stuck with me, and I usually conquered it by bringing order to chaos. Maybe the disarray of the suite bugged me more than I thought. I could get up and straighten the room. No, that'd wake Audrey. She'd needed some rest.

My six-oh family brought the jerks to justice, so my nerves should stop firing like pyromaniacs on July Fourth. Audrey might not care if she lost her job, but if she was somehow responsible for hurting her family's business…what if they blamed her? Heck, poor Rick didn't deserve my dad targeting him. I couldn't just let it happen. I'd go home tomorrow and talk to Dad. No matter what kind of deal I made with him, this would be my last con. He didn't seem to care for Audrey all that much either.

I cradled Audrey closer and felt her slight movement with each breath accompanied by a little sniffle. The nagging worry wound through every part of me until I couldn't deny it any more. This could be the last time I held her.

22

Audrey

My face felt sweaty, my jaw cocked at a weird angle. I opened my eyes, and yawning, settled back into myself. Kyle had wrapped his arms around mine to keep me warm from the air conditioner in the con suite, but his one arm dropped away whenever he had fallen asleep. His head pressed against my cheek, and a little trail of drool pooled onto his costume. He looked so peaceful. I kept my body completely still so I could watch him dream whatever vision that made him smile like that.

The disappointment of losing the contest faded with rest. Winning had been a long shot. It was stupid to get my hopes up so high, to think I could dig Uncle Rick out of his hole. I couldn't give him any money, but I could still upsell my butt off at work later. I'd try harder. Maybe I could do some free advertising online and I'd help with the neighborhood protest against Mega Mart, which really was the big problem. Uncle Rick could earn back his loan with sales as long as the store still existed, right?

Me and Kyle were cooped up in the corner of a messy suite, due to add to the con funk with how badly we both needed showers, but the morning couldn't have been brighter. It was a perfect imperfect moment engraved into my memory. Waves of tingles saturated throughout me like my body had learned a new sense as tangible as touch and taste. How had I lived without experiencing this? Kyle's dad tried to keep him down, but he rose above it. He chased after those guys, he went on stage, he called the six-oh, all for me. Kyle meant more than some boy in a costume, a handful of pleasant hours, or a kind deed. I couldn't even name what he was.

"Hey, check the volunteer list for the panels in main programming." A girl carrying a clipboard entered the suite, followed by a few other staffers wearing bright orange badges.

Kyle bolted up, eyes wide. He caught his breath. "Guess I fell asleep."

"Yeah, me too," I said.

One of the newly arrived staffers glanced toward us. "You two have any shifts soon? We need someone down in registration."

I shook my head. "Nawh, just need a couple more hours to crash. We'll get out of your way."

Kyle groaned as he stood. I joined him in his pain. The same pins and needles filled my numb legs, and we both hobbled out of the room. As we fell in step down the hall, his hand found mine without thought.

I held him tight. "I have to work the booth until the con closes. Sunday markdown deals are like blood in the water for a feeding frenzy. I'm sorry…"

"No, do your job. You can make more money for your uncle and stuff."

I nodded, squeezing his hand harder.

He sighed heavily and zoned out at his feet while we walked. What was he thinking about? Friday night he'd acted weird, too. Was it something that happened with his dad?

"Is anything wrong?" I clutched my helmet a little tighter.

He pressed the button to call the elevator. "I think I need to go home now. Shouldn't stay too much longer."

The happy tingle wrenched into annoyance. "Better not be because your dad's guilt-tripped you into leaving again. You'll be eighteen next year. He can't run your life forever."

Kyle's mouth turned down. He looked at the floor, shifting his weight in a weird way.

Was he trying to guilt *me* now? "Hey, you can't…"

He turned his head, water rising in his eyes. "I'm sorry. I'm so sorry." He inhaled a shaky breath. "I need to go try and talk my dad down. I don't think he'll follow through. Probably just wanted to scare me."

The elevator dinged and swooshed open. He took a step, but I grabbed his arm. "What's going on?"

"Tell you later." He tried to move into the elevator. I yanked him back, and the doors closed.

My fingers began to tremble. No, not now. With a deep breath, I banished the shakes and unwanted thoughts. I needed facts. "Tell me."

He rested his hand on the one I had grabbing his arm and led me out of the way of the doors. "Friday night when I came back, Dad had made a threat. I couldn't stomach it, that he'd actually say something or do something so crazy just to get me to leave the con."

I nodded. "What was it?"

"His law firm handles Mega Mart, and he said the case in Dallas could go either way. He insinuated he'd make sure Mega Mart got the location where *Infinity* is right now, ya know, if I defied him." He paused. "Which I did."

"Are you serious?" My jaw dropped, and all the mental gymnastics in the world couldn't keep me from freaking out. I started to shake.

Kyle peeled my hand away and wrapped his arms around me. "Don't worry. I'll fix it. I won't let him do that on purpose. Maybe he can sway them to use the other site instead. I can get him to try."

"How?"

"Give him what he wants."

"But you just found out you love this. Even the contest, the six-oh saved us, and…" Of course we'd never get to see each other without these weekend retreats. He lived too far away, we were still in high school, and we both had jobs. Once we started college, it'd be different, but that was so far away.

He sighed. "I know. But, I don't know another way out of it. Can't let him target you or Uncle Rick."

I leaned my head against the wall by the elevator, looking up at blank ceiling. "I don't want him to keep controlling you. You deserve more. And I…I want…" I dropped my chin to see his eyes squeezed shut. It hurt him, too. Damn it. "We're not over. This isn't over. Let him think he's won the battle, but we'll win the war."

"What do you mean?" He opened his eyes.

"Tell him what he wants. I'll find a time to see you, and we can figure something else out. Buy us some time."

Kyle cradled his helmet as he thought. "He always seems to see through me."

"We can try."

A small smile tugged his lips. "Okay. I'll try."

The elevator dinged again, but once we got on, he'd leave. Who knew when we'd get to see each other again. "Let's take the stairs."

Just like our glacial dinner when we rescued his car, we could drag out every last second to its fullest. We disappeared into the stairwell, once again finding a private world in a public place. Plush hotel carpet dulled the sounds of our descent. It was quiet. Quiet meant thinking. Thinking meant missing him, and he wasn't even gone yet.

Kyle stopped on the landing, and his gaze flickered from my one eye to the other. His breath hitched. "I never told you. Thank you…for making a costume to go with mine."

It probably seemed silly or stupid to most people, but he got it. He got me. Making the bounty hunter wasn't about cosplaying, photoshoots, contests, or cosplay drama. I wanted to connect to him. He understood.

"I didn't know how else to say what I wanted…"

He opened his mouth, but remained silent. Instead he leaned close, and our lips met. He kissed me, gentle and slow, like we had to fully experience every moment.

I put my arms behind him, pressing his plastic armor into me while I hugged him closer, tighter, longer. I'd never release. He couldn't go home if I didn't let him out of my hold. Gentle kisses turned desperate as he embraced me tighter.

My damned stuffy nose wouldn't take in enough air. We broke apart, and I breathed hard and deep. Kyle had to catch his breath, too, his face red.

I laughed. We'd almost suffocated each other.

Kyle smiled only for a few seconds. "I'll see you again."

"I know."

He glanced down the stairs. "I need to go. If I stay with you, I won't leave."

I gave him a hug for the road. "Drive safely."

"I will."

Kyle turned and hurried down the remaining stairs. In another blink, he disappeared out the door. My heart hammered, trying desperately to stifle the wave surging through me. I wouldn't cry. I'd see him again.

Why didn't I believe it?

I stood outside the dealers' room while cosplayers and fans of all kinds waited for the doors to open. Wired attendees talked too loud for morning ears, con funk grew to impressive levels of stink, and everything continued as it usually did. But I sat on the sidelines, apart from the energy hovering in the air. Now that Kyle had left, a hollow bubble followed me around. I'd gotten used to holding his hand.

Time for another shift working the booth, and hopefully this'd be a record-breaking Sunday. A gaggle of waiting patrons swarmed closer to the ballroom doors, so I snuck past them to the loading dock entrance. The staffer checked my badge and waved me inside.

On the back row, Dan was already rearranging the buttons, pins, and jewelry on the table. My shoulders fell, giving my strong bounty hunter a pitiful profile. I hadn't seen him for more than two seconds since last week when he gave me the cold shoulder. He switched off shifts when I came to work yesterday. He'd probably keep avoiding me. He'd gotten pretty damn good at it.

I lifted my head, hidden behind the mask, and marched to the booth. The instant Dan caught me in his line of sight, he bolted through the curtain.

"Oh no, not today," Uncle Rick said, loud enough they might've heard him outside.

An exasperated Dan was shoved back into the booth as I walked up. Uncle Rick shook his head. "I'm done watching this nonsense. You two talk it out, and don't come back until I can work in a peaceful environment. Got it?"

Dan vaulted over the corner of the table into the aisle beside me. "Yeah. Got it." He glanced at me then looked away. "Come on. You heard him."

I followed Dan past the last booth to the false wall on the side of the ballroom toward the loading area. We ducked through the exit door and into the narrow hall. Part of me felt weird for being forced back there with him, but the better part sighed in relief. Maybe he'd listen to me. Maybe we could work through this?

Dan crossed his arms and chewed his lip, his gaze avoiding my face. Or really, my helmet. With that barrier between us, we couldn't have a real conversation.

I removed the helmet. "I don't like you being so angry with me," I actually said the words out loud. All my filters and walls had broken when my costume got smashed. One good thing came of it.

He kicked the false wall with his heel over and over. The little drumbeat echoed his agitated mood, nonsensical rhythm and everything. Maybe that's why he didn't join band with me in middle school.

"I'm not really *mad* at you. I just…I dunno." He sighed.

My fingers tapped the inside rim of the helmet, fast, slow, and fast again. "This sucks. I miss talking with you. Why does it have to be so weird? Can't we be friends?"

"Only ever just friends…"

My heart squeezed as if I'd wrung it dry. "I never wanted to hurt you."

He nodded and his chin dropped again. "I know. I didn't mean to be such an ass either. It just sorta happened."

"Uh huh. You've never apologized for teasing me before." I razzed, and he half-chuckled in response. "So, is the awkward over now? Can we be normal again, please?"

His drumming on the wall stopped. Quiet and noisy at the same time, the loading dock hall felt eerily familiar. The last time, things began to get weird. Maybe now, we'd fix it. Please let us fix it.

"Dan?"

He took a breath, yanked the helmet from my grip, and popped it on his head. He made a fart noise. "Next time, I put a real stinker in here before giving it back."

I tried to grab the helmet, but he twisted out of the way. "Hey, I need that."

He lifted the bottom of the mask and stuck out his tongue. "Looks better on me, sucka!"

"Come on, we gotta get back to work. The bargain buyers are chomping at the bit." I swiped for it again, and he ran a few feet down the hall, laughing—really laughing.

The weight lifted from me I didn't recognize was there. Lighter and freer, I let everything go. I wrestled with Dan and had to resort to my classic cheat. A quick tickle in his armpit and he surrendered my helmet, and as he pulled it off, he smiled. Maybe we could go back to being friends. It'd make things easier on Uncle Rick, too.

Dan's eyebrows twisted, and he pointed at me. "What happened to your costume?"

My hand automatically covered the broken edge on the front piece. He obviously didn't watch the contest last night. "A couple of guys tore it up."

"What?" He dropped the helmet, grabbed my shoulders, and glanced around my back where he'd see the worst part of the damage. "How? When?" He stopped. "Are you okay?"

I nodded. "Fine. Right before the contest last night. We didn't win the prize for you guys. I'm sorry."

Dan exhaled through his teeth, making a loud whistle. "That's fine. I'm just glad you weren't hurt. I…if I wasn't being a jackass…"

"It's okay, really. Kyle stopped them from doing more."

"Right." He jerked his hands off my shoulders, and they found their way back into his pockets. He leaned against the wall.

I picked up the helmet, holding it between us. "Security expelled the guys responsible. Kyle called—"

"No, please." Dan stood straight and moved to the center of the hall. "We just got back to normal, and I can't do it. I can't if you keep bringing him up. You wanna be 'friends,' then Boba Fett dude is off limits. To me, pretend he doesn't exist."

"Dan…"

He sighed. "Please? I just can't handle it. Not yet."

"Okay, my lips are sealed."

Dan put on a smile and nodded toward the exit. "I'm glad you're okay. For now, we gotta get to work."

He left first, and I followed slowly behind as he sped over to the booth. Uncle Rick was facing the side with a blue zippered pouch opened in his hands. He frowned and closed it up. Good sales for one weekend wouldn't fill the pit in his ledgers. Since I couldn't give him money, I could improve the webpage for the neighborhood petition and advertise it around town. I lost the contest, but maybe I could help save the store. Webpages were more my forte than craftsmanship anyway.

23

Kyle

I gripped the steering wheel, breathed steadily, and focused on driving the boring trek to Waco. The taste of Audrey's kiss clung to my lips. I could still feel the pressure of her holding me, as if we hadn't separated. I seized the feeling, pulling it around me like a blanket that I could keep close forever.

Buttcrack-early on Sunday meant light traffic and a short trip home. I pulled up to the house and parked by the curb. The garage door was down, the lights off, and though Dad could be sleeping in, my gut threw off massive "something's wrong" warnings. No point in dawdling, so I forged onward and went inside.

The dark foyer, living room, kitchen, and stairway projected a deafening silence. Even my sneakers made no sound as I crossed from room to room. Dad wasn't home. I'd been in the house alone a lot, so why'd it feel like the preview to a slasher flick? I rubbed an imagined chill from my arms.

The foreboding atmosphere followed me to my room. I sat on my bed, surrounded by the soothing presence of the comforter Mom had given me. My stomach growled, half from hunger and half from stupid guilt-worry-fear vying for dominance in there. So far, fear was in a commanding lead. Where the heck was Dad? Would I be able to change his mind?

A loud *bang* from a door echoed downstairs. Dad must be home. I scooted off the bed and hobbled for a few feet as blood reentered my legs. The negotiations in my stomach increased in fury, worry taking the forefront with guilt lagging behind. I almost puked. Why didn't I eat something? How could I bring up the problem with Audrey's store when I had a sixty percent chance of throwing up?

I somehow got outside my room and down the stairs. Dad was preheating the oven for lunch.

"Dad?" I waited for the inevitable.

He turned, regarding me with neither a frown nor a clenched jaw. His face seemed relaxed, as did his posture. He pressed start on the oven. "Do you want pepperoni or Hawaiian?"

I stared, stock still. Where was the explosion? I had more than talked back, I defied him. He never let me get away with even a sarcastic aside, but now he was acting calm and rational? Had he already done something? Gut check—correction, eighty percent chance.

Dad walked to the fridge and opened the freezer. "I'll heat up both. We can have leftovers tomorrow."

"Sure…" I inhaled. "Dad?"

He slid the pizzas into the oven and looked up.

"I'm sorry. You were right about everything. I shoulda gone home with you Friday." I backed out of the way as he crossed the kitchen

Dad grabbed two paper plates from the drawer. "Yeah?"

"I promise. I won't dress up again. So please, will you try to keep Mega Mart from tearing down Audrey's store? Her uncle's livelihood is at stake. Mega Mart has a billion dollars. They don't need that specific site." I grabbed the back of the kitchen chair as an anchor.

"You want me to use my influence to sway a client for personal reasons?"

I swallowed a ball of phlegm. Ninety percent chance. "You…you said you were gonna before."

Dad nodded. "It's a big deal. I will influence the decision, but only if I can be sure you're gonna step in line."

All I could do was nod.

"You have to toss that costume. I'll watch you do it." He set the paper plates on the table and turned back to the counter to grab the napkin holder.

An actual cramp made bile rise, and I choked it down. The culmination of five years of birthday money and hundreds of tutoring hours, that costume put me back seven hundred dollars. I'd made it bigger in case I grew another inch, which was theoretically possible. The friends, no the family I made in the six-oh, what would happen with that? Could I still hang with them? Would I throw all that away, too?

But Audrey…if I didn't, she'd blame herself for whatever happened to Uncle Rick. I had to. "Okay." I gripped the chair harder until the wooden bar dug into my palm.

Dad rolled back his shoulders and heaved a sigh. The corners of his eyes seemed to droop. "There's one more thing, Son. You've been disobedient since you met that girl, lying to me, running off to get on *stage* wearing that crap." He set the napkins on the table. "You can't see her anymore."

"Dad!" I almost took down the chair, but let go. "You can't—"

"It's up to you, Kyle. You want to be the man in charge? You have a decision and you'll have to face the consequences." He spoke with the same tone someone would use to relate the weather. He'd made up his mind, and if I didn't play the game, I'd lose. Audrey would lose.

Either way, I'd lose her.

Her voice rose over the horrid chatter in my head. *We're not over. This isn't over. Let him think he's won the battle, but we'll win the war.* I didn't have to keep the promise. I could get her back eventually, right?

My mouth formed the words. "I won't see her again. Please, just save her uncle's store."

Dad made a weak smile and patted me on the back, which made my stomach tip the scales. I choked it down.

He said, "Thank you. Once you throw away the costume, I'll go to my office and make the calls." The oven beeped. "Twelve minutes until dinner."

I turned toward the kitchen door. "I'm not hungry. We're low on snacks, so I'm gonna head out for awhile."

The next moment took me out the front door, and in a surreal out-of-body event, I jumped into the car and turned the key at the same time. I had to escape, if only for an evening. Maybe Garrett could help me figure a way out. I could plan some way to meet up with Audrey, and he could cover, or something. Anything. There had to be a way.

After driving around for fifteen minutes, I pulled up to the curb by Garrett's house. I'd only been there once after JROTC, but it stood out in my memory at the end of a cul-de-sac. He didn't need me bothering him, but…where else could I go? I'd drive to Josh's or one of my six-oh friends', but none of them lived remotely close. The car only had a quarter tank left.

Lights flicked on in the upstairs window, Garrett's room. It was a sign.

The smell of freshly cut lawn tickled my nose. I sneezed and walked around the edges up the driveway to the stoop. The hollow sound of the doorbell rang way too loud. A minute later, the handle jiggled, and Garrett opened the door, wearing a black polo with a d20 stitched on it.

"Kyle? Hey, everything okay?" He waved me in.

I shook my head and closed the door. We continued to stand in the entryway, and he didn't really move to invite me further in. Maybe he was busy today, just my luck.

"So, what's the deal?" he asked.

"Fight with my dad. I need some time away. Maybe we could dig into an MMO or something for a few hours?" Thumbs hooked into my pockets, I pressed my fingers to my thighs.

Garrett put his weight on one leg, which made him lean a bit to the side. "What'd he do?"

"Being himself times a thousand. Never noticed how he orchestrated everything before now. I dunno, I guess I needed time away to think." It felt like I was freefalling, just standing by the front door with nothing around me but the pile of shoes on the tile.

"Ahh…okay." His weight shifted again. Slight movements and nervous tics piled upon one another.

I couldn't stand it anymore. "Can I come in for a while?"

"I wanna help you out, but I'm really busy today. I'm sorry. Things probably aren't as bad as you're thinking."

Something weighed me down all over. My hands, feet, chest, all seemed to pull me to the tile, trapping me without escape. "No, it is that bad. I can't go home."

"Dude, I'm sorry. I wish I could help."

The weight settled deep in my body like I'd separated from the real world into a space truly on my own. "You're seriously 'too busy'?"

He reached behind me and opened the door. "Your dad's made it clear I can't cover for you anymore. He keeps calling me every time you run off. I mean, don't you have a closer friend he can harass?"

His admission hit me in the chest like a fist. I did have closer friends, brothers, but I thought I could count him among them. "Yeah. Sorry."

"See you at school." Garrett put his hand on my shoulder, though I couldn't feel it.

Then I was outside on the concrete steps alone, silent, and trapped by an inescapable truth. I could avoid it, but I couldn't be free.

Even if there was nowhere to go, I'd put off going home as long as possible, so I toured the outskirts of the city, walked the mall, ate a fast food burger that tasted like cardboard, and drove until the gas light came on. I spent another hour sitting on the swings in the park until it got way too creepy. By the time I parked in the driveway, it had to be close to midnight. The clock in the dash was always wrong.

Time to face him.

I grabbed my phone from the passenger seat. Then I sucked in a breath, pushing strength into my feet, and marched up the driveway. On either side, campaign signs reading "Vote Cole Porter, City Council" pierced the grass like banners with family crests, marking the entrance to his kingdom.

Dad was standing on the stoop, arms crossed. "Where did you go?"

"Nowhere."

"Dammit, Kyle, you can't just rabbit off and disappear. You didn't answer my texts or my call. What was I supposed to think?" He shook his head. "Why do you keep doing this to me, Son? How can you be so selfish?"

Was I really that selfish? All I wanted was one hobby I could call mine, friends I could count on, a girl who liked me. That wasn't too much, was it? Dad's worn frown made my body react with the pangs of guilt like a Pavlovian response.

He was doing it on purpose.

"I just wanna do one thing for myself. Can't I?" I pleaded, honest-to-God begged. I probably sounded pathetic. "Please. I won't run off again, but let me see Audrey..."

Dad uncrossed his arms, letting them hang heavy at his sides. "You're making things harder on yourself." He walked to my car, opened the passenger door, and popped the trunk with the switch in the glovebox. Before I could think, he'd gotten out the box with my costume.

I felt hollow, like my bones were made of wood. He waved me over, and I walked without commanding my own limbs. A gesture, a glance, a well-placed word, they pulled my strings and I obeyed.

Dad dropped the box at my feet. "Toss it."

My numb hands hoisted the box and carried it to the curb. They opened the plastic lid of the garbage bin, dumping the contents of the box. Seven. Hundred. Dollars. The only thing I'd truly worked for…trash.

I broke down the empty cardboard box and tossed it into the accompanying recycle bin, pivoted, and marched back to the driveway. Eyes forward, chin up, I stared past Dad's head into the dark street beyond. Empty.

"Phone. Keys."

I followed orders, placing them into his opened palm.

Dad inhaled deeply. "I changed the password on the alarm. You'll take the bus to school and do your homework in the living room—I'm taking your computer. I'll pick you up from tutoring. Is that clear?"

"Until when?" I had to ask, though it hardly mattered now.

"Until you fall in line."

Without my phone, car, or even laptop, I really had no way to contact Audrey. She'd programed her number into my phone, but it's not like I memorized it. How could I plan a meetup if I couldn't talk to her? She was wrong. We lost the battle *and* the war. Before I knew it, I had found my way back into my room. Neat rows of books, perfectly made bed, and all my things put away where they went. My sanctuary had become my prison.

24

Audrey

Someone knocked three times on my bedroom door. I pulled my drying eyes away from the monitor. I'd been digging through the internet for, what, over an hour? At least I found some supporting information about Mega Mart that could help Uncle Rick. Getting it up on the website was top priority.

Another knock. "Audrey?"

Sara? I opened the door. She was wearing a tank top with little Rebel logos all over, the one I got her for Christmas. It was a hidden type of "geeky," but she wore it out anyway. She really was trying to reconnect.

"What'cha doin' home?" I asked.

"The stars have aligned. We're actually going to have dinner together. Mom says the chicken parm is almost done." And as soon as she said it, the delicious smell of breaded chicken and absurd amounts of cheese wafted into the room.

I shook my head. I couldn't let the mouth-watering thought of dinner distract me. "Well I'll eat in my room. I've got research to do for Uncle Rick's protest." I turned away from the door, but left it open.

Sara came inside behind me. "Oh. I hope it's going well."

"Fine…I guess." I went back to the computer and typed into the search bar without bothering to sit down.

"Hey, you do realize I'm here to see you, right?" She sat down on my bed, bouncing a couple of times.

What she said only half registered. "Yeah…"

Sara appeared beside me, waving her hand in front of my face. "What's got you all distracted?"

"I'm worried about Uncle Rick, so I'm…what? What's that look?" I watched her mouth twist and eyes roll, her version of *yeah right*. "Well I…"

Of course I was worried about Uncle Rick, Dan, Aunt Jill, and the fate of their store. I had to get sources to show Mega Mart moving into the neighborhood was a bad deal. Right?

She returned to her spot on the bed, cocking her head to the side. "Come on. What's going on?"

As she asked, an ache pulled from inside, and Kyle's face popped into my head. I could busy myself all I wanted, but I couldn't forget the real thing on my mind. "It'll sound dumb."

She waved me over to sit next to her. "Try me."

I flumped onto the bed much harder than she had. "There's this cosplayer who does a bounty hunter, and he does it to honor his mom. I used that money to make a costume to match his for this last con because his psycho dad might not let me see him again. It sucks. I really like him." The words rushed out in a torrent. "I know it's stupid, but I thought it was really important to do this. I haven't heard from him since he got home Sunday morning. I'm worried…really worried."

"It's not dumb." Sara leaned to the side and put her arm around my shoulders.

My chest constricted, and I suddenly felt like crying. I tried to be so strong, to hold it in and hold it up, but I couldn't. Tears beaded in my eyes. "What if I never see Kyle again? I can't imagine that. I think…I think I love him."

"Oh, Aud." She squeezed me and rested her head on my shoulder. "If he feels like you do, I'm sure it'll work out somehow."

"I hope you're right." I leaned against her. For a split second, we were little kids again, sitting on the bottom bunk our first time away at camp. I had gotten homesick, and she made me feel safe. Whatever stupid crap that pulled us apart a few years ago hadn't dissolved that glue that comes from growing up together.

It sounded like she sighed, not as if she were annoyed, but relieved in some way. A little chuckle breathed near my ear. "So, Kyle, huh? What's he like?"

I snickered. "Dinner's almost ready. There's not enough time."

"Guess I'm staying after. I want all the details."

The clamp on my heart released. That's what was missing. I'd have a chance to talk about Kyle, and even better, I'd get to really talk to Sara. We'd patch up the rifts between us, one conversation at a time. Bit by bit.

"Come on, let's get some of that dinner before my stomach leaps out Alien-style." I got off the bed and opened the door.

Last night, uneasy dreams had filled whatever sleep I did get, and I spent my hours of insomnia trying to help Uncle Rick's petition. If only that was what had kept me up.

My cheek stuck to the glass case, breath rippling a fog across the surface. Only one customer had come in since I started my shift. I lifted my head and clicked on my phone. Still nothing, nada, zilch. I texted Kyle like thirty times. It'd been a whole week. Why hadn't he sent something back, anything? I'd settle for a *still alive*, or even an emoji.

Tinkling bells jolted me from worried thoughts. A tall man in a gray suit walked straight through the store to my register. He carried a leather briefcase in his left hand. Did Uncle Rick hire a lawyer after all?

"Oh, I'm sorry. The owner isn't in right now. I can take a message." I pulled a stack of Post-its out of the drawer below the register.

He set the briefcase on the counter. "No need. I'm here to see you, Miss Warren."

The voice sent ice water through my veins. Kyle's dad. Why didn't I recognize him at first? "Oh, uh, okay…" I stepped back to put a few more inches between us.

"You don't need to be nervous. I apologize for how I came across the last time. The situation is complicated." He slid a business card over the glass, his arm casting a shadow on the collectibles in the case.

When he pulled his hand away, I retrieved the card. It read "Cole Porter: Attorney at Law" followed by his email and phone number. "I don't…why are you here?"

Mr. Porter gestured to the empty store behind him. "I hear this business is in litigation and that you have personal connections with the owner and his family?"

Oh no, he had to be here because of what Kyle said. He was going to make sure the store lost its home. I took another step backward, my butt sticking halfway into the stockroom.

"I want to help you, Miss Warren." He smiled. "Although my client has sights on this parcel of land, they have another option in a neighboring suburb should this fall through. I've counseled them about the location in Waco, and they're grateful for my insight. I fully believe they'd be inclined to take my suggestion to avoid the controversy at this site and take the easier option."

I stared at his unreadable face. Last time, he looked so angry. "What? Why?" I coughed. "I mean, of course that would be amazing, but I still don't know why you'd do that for us?"

He rolled back his shoulders to grow even taller. "I'm not offering this help for free. I need you to do something for me in return."

"What can I do? I don't have—"

"Simple. I want you out of Kyle's life. If you break it off with him, I'll help save Mr. Grayson's business, and I'll throw in monetary compensation for you as well."

"What?" The world swam. I grabbed the doorjamb to steady myself.

"I'll tell you what," Kyle's dad said. "I don't like you. You're a bad influence on my son. If you don't take this deal, you still ain't seeing him again."

He waved his hand like he was thinking. "You're likely just a high school crush. Don't you think it's important for a father to bond with his son?"

I blinked, my mouth hung open like a gasping fish. Now he wanted to control me, too? "If that's what you want, you should get to know the kid you have instead of the one you wish you did."

"I knew I didn't like you." He lifted his chin. "You're done with Kyle. Break it off, and you get to save this pathetic store. Don't, and Mega Mart will fight like a rodeo bull fresh from the pen. The legal expenses and filings will put Mr. Grayson out of business well before they tear down this crappy strip mall."

My knees weakened, and my eyes lost focus as I forgot to breathe. Blackmail? I couldn't throw Uncle Rick and them under the bus just to keep seeing Kyle. That'd be the selfish choice. I had changed.

I tried to respond, but my mouth wouldn't work. It just twitched beginnings of unformed words.

"Tell him something like 'this situation is too stressful' and you can't handle it. Say that you're too young to deal with his baggage," he said.

"But...but I..." A hard lump lodged in my neck, or my chest, something unreal that stopped me from breathing. But I could breathe, I just couldn't answer. I didn't have an answer. Kyle's dad laid it all out very clear.

He tilted his chin, leveling his gaze with mine. "You're just kids. Ain't like this little relationship was going long term anyway, and if you do this now, you can save Mr. Grayson's family some hardship."

The words made sense on the outside, all logical and objective. But when I had met Kyle, a hum of energy took root around my heart, and it wasn't ready to leave. I loved him. I knew what I felt. How could I throw away something so unbelievable?

Kyle's dad grabbed the handle of his briefcase and slid it off the counter so it swung down by his side. "I got work to do. What is your answer?"

Uncle Rick, Aunt Jill, and Dan were in a rough spot. They weren't my responsibility, really...but, but if they lost their house when I could help them? What if Dan found out? He hated Kyle anyway. He'd never forgive me.

"I'm sorry I couldn't help you. I hope you don't regret your decision." Kyle's dad heaved a sigh and turned.

"Wait!" It popped out before I could stop it.

"Yes?" He turned his head.

"Fine. Okay. What do I have to do?"

He set the briefcase on the counter, opened it, and retrieved a piece of paper. He handed it over. "Go on to the house. Kyle is already home. Call this number and put your phone in your pocket, so I can hear what you tell him. When you break it off, you must not mention our deal. He can't know I had anything to do with it. You blame yourself, got it?"

"Got it." I crumpled the paper into my pocket. "How do I know you'll keep your side of the deal?"

"I'm not in the business of lying to get my way, though you taught my son well enough. I'll contact my client as soon as you end your call. Should take about a week to get the appropriate meetings set up, and then they'll announce the new building site." He took his stuff and gave me a little nod. "Goodbye, Miss Warren."

Then Mr. Asshole left, and instead of the worrisome feeling of emptiness, the store filled with a slick aura as if his attitude left a gross film over everything. The merchandise felt tainted, and I felt disgusting. How could I follow through with this and let Kyle know I didn't mean any of it? He could get hurt. He could hate me. Or I could throw away the opportunity to help and Dan would hate me.

Me. All about *me* again. I couldn't give into my selfish desires to protect what I wanted. This time, I really would put them first.

I flopped forward, draping my arms over the case and hitting my chin into the glass. It sucked. It all sucked. At least I didn't have a store full of shoppers to see me sulk about it.

Kyle

My face buried further into the worn fibers of my *Star Wars* comforter, which smelled of childhood and safety. I inhaled. If I banished everything else, the soft shelter resurrected faint images of my mother. A broad smile flickered behind my eyelids, and long fingers enveloped my small hand. I hadn't forgotten her, not completely. Warm memories stirred recent feelings—Audrey. Did she assume I was grounded? Or was she mad because I hadn't contacted her?

All I wanted to do was get out of the house. Dad was in a funk again, so even though he'd gotten me to "stay in line," it wasn't good enough. I couldn't drag him up from the pit any more than I could hoist myself out of it. We were stuck in it together, me and Dad. He got what he wanted. I had only him to rely on, and he could use that to make my life a perfect echo of his. Why hadn't I seen it before? Why'd it take me so long? Dad's concern had warped beyond reason. The second I got a clue, I lost what little freedom I had.

Downstairs, the doorbell rang a few times. Dad wasn't home, and I wasn't in the mood to deal with solicitors. I closed my eyes, trying to reclaim the fleeting thoughts and escape into the good parts of the past. The connection fizzled and was gone, just like Mom. Just like Audrey.

It rang again. Someone pounded on the front door. Another ring. What could be so important? I rubbed my eyes and slugged downstairs with a yawn.

I opened it just in time to duck a knock toward the face.

"Oh, sorry. Sorry!" Audrey cringed.

"What? How?" I glanced toward the garage and to the street. No sign of Dad's truck. "Are you crazy?"

She dug her hands into her pockets, avoiding my eyes. "Can I come inside?"

"Ye…yeah. Come on in." I moved to the side and closed the door behind her. Audrey popping up at my house out of nowhere was weird, a good weird, but something made my little arm hairs stand on end.

"I like your house. Big TV, nice." She took her hands from her pockets and held them together, fidgeting with the waistband of her jeans. "Can I see your room?"

"Uh, sure."

I guided her up the steps, creaking wood showing its age. Audrey looked around at the wallpaper, toward the ceiling, but she never looked right at me. Her fingers twisted around each other in constant motion.

We relocated to my room, and as a soon as her eyes popped anime wide, a full-body blush took hold of me. Big mistake. What in the multiverse was I thinking?

She grinned at my childish bedspread, the *Star Wars* posters, and the neurotically alphabetized bookshelf of neatness. She'd think I was nutty. Why did I okay going to my room? *Idiot, Kyle. Idiot!*

I shoved my hands into my jeans. "This must be weird. We can go anywhere else, now."

Audrey shook her head. "Please, I want to stay here just a minute. I have to go soon anyway." Her voice trailed off.

"Oh, okay." As long as she didn't focus too hard on the fact I arranged the action figures by chronological introduction.

She wasn't obsessing over my meticulous organization. The tightness in her face seemed scary serious. "There's no easy way to explain this."

My stomach formed a hardened ball in my abdomen. "Explain what?"

"There's so much going on. You live all the way down here, and every time we see each other it's like you're Han trapped in carbonite. I don't know that I'll ever see you again. I can't keep doing things, like this."

"Wait…what're you saying?" The sick feeling flooded my entire being so forcefully, I nearly hurled all over the freshly cleaned floor. She couldn't really mean it. Could she?

Audrey finally chose to look me in the eye. Her gaze locked. She put her hand on her heart and winked. "I can't see you anymore, *like this*. I want you to understand. I really thought you were the Han to my Leia, but even Lando screwed it all up for them. I'm sorry. I really am."

Only Audrey would break up with me with references to the thing I loved more than anything. Except her. My body went into panic-mode—sweaty palms, dry throat, and near paralysis of my brain.

"You're kidding, right?" My voice cracked into falsetto.

She glanced at the corners of the room, then stared at the shelf with a frown. She turned back to me, chewing her glitz-less lips. "Han and Leia had a long break before she rescued him, but I can't handle that. I can't go two weeks with no word, only to hope I'll see you then. It's just not going to work."

"It was only *one* week." I reclaimed my normal register. "Dad locked up my phone. I'll find some other way. Maybe Josh would—"

"You don't get it." She grabbed my hand and squeezed, hard. "I can't be *your Leia*. This is goodbye." Her eyes were dry as her gaze bore into me like a drill. She didn't look upset, but confident like when she played her roles.

Shouldn't she be at least a little sad? Didn't she care? Maybe I was the only one who fell so deep…who fell at all.

My breath hitched. "No, I don't get it."

"You will." She squeezed my hand again, and her fingers lingered behind, leaving the electricity of her touch to torture me.

In another second she had left. I stood on my vacuumed carpet alone in my cell. Once upon a time, the control I possessed over my room gave me solace. What a lie. It meant nothing, *did* nothing.

I went to the shelf and tossed books to the floor, opened drawers and flung my clothes everywhere. T-shirts landed in a heap, jeans sprawled across the desk, and action figures fell to their deaths in a pile of clutter. I became a tornado in my tidy room, tearing all my careful work to pieces.

Useless. Pointless. Why try.

I leaned backward until I dropped flat onto the bed. The popcorn ceiling no longer hid an alien landscape as it blurred through my tears. They didn't fall, just pooled over my eyes to create a mess of white and gray. Another mess.

Closing my eyes, I repeated algebra expressions I knew from heart. I saw equations, x equals negative b, plus or minus the square root of b squared minus four a c, all over two a. I fell asleep.

A pounding headache forced me to get up, sticky goop in my eyes. I yawned, and reconnected with reality. My clothes lay in a pile, all the stuff from my shelves scattered on top and across the floor. The air sucked out of my lungs. My hands shook.

Audrey.

Next thing I knew, I was sliding books back onto the shelf, and as I put things away, the breakup played in my mind again. Audrey had seemed worried, though not upset. She should've felt bad like me. *Like this.*

Her voice had been awkward, too, like she took little pauses before saying certain things. I did that when tutoring to call attention to the key tricks for solving a problem, or when I was trying to hint for the student to do a certain step first. I repeated things.

Like this.

She'd said, "I can't keep doing things *like this*. I can't see you anymore, *like this*." And she kept bringing up *Star Wars*. I never had a girl break up with me before, but it didn't feel at all right. Something was wrong.

The lights came on in my skull. Holy cow, she had been speaking in code? Dad must have put her up to it. He must have been listening in, and she'd been searching for cameras with all those fidgety glances.

I sat up and closed my eyes. What did she say exactly? Something about Han and Leia and carbonite. There was a reference to *my Leia*, bounty hunter Leia. She'd rescued Han; Audrey planned to rescue me. Holy shit, in two weeks. What would happen in two weeks?

Running through my phone calendar in my head, all that stood out was Austin Comic Con. I'd need to create an alibi.

I exhaled, releasing tension with the air. A code, ha ha! Dad's stubborn refusal to watch *Star Wars* might've saved us. A surge a triumph welled up inside. He tried to control us. He thought he had all the power and knew all the rules, but we played him. It was our game, now.

I sat in the kitchen, shoveling sugary cinnamon bites into my mouth and hunching over the table. My eyes hurt from rubbing them raw. They looked good, red lids and bloodshot all through the white parts. Heck, almost looked like a zombie. Must remember that trick for a *Walking Dead* cosplay.

All these years, Dad had used subtle cues to get me to do what he wanted. How hard could it be?

The front door shut loudly, and scuffling came from the living room as Dad put away his briefcase. The alarm system beeped, and a robotic voice chirped, "System armed, stay." After ensuring the cage was locked, Dad crossed into the kitchen and paused—silent.

Good, look what you've done, jerk. Feel bad about it.

"Cereal for supper?" Dad asked, feigning ignorance.

"Didn't have ice cream. This was the best I could do." I chomped another convincing bite and turned to look him straight on with my zombie eyeballs.

He put on a frown. Maybe he genuinely felt bad, but now I couldn't tell. From now on, I'd always second guess.

"What happened?" He asked.

I slammed the spoon into the bowl. "I got dumped. She broke up with me because she couldn't handle my 'situation.' Hope you're happy."

"I'm sorry. I know you feel bad right now, but it's probably for the best."

"Yeah right." I scraped the chair as I stood. Anger boiled through me, heating my face; I wasn't acting anymore. "Looking at you is making it worse. I'm fixing to call Aunt Beth and see if I can get some time away."

Dad said, "You better not be thinking of hauling off to one of those conventions again."

I rolled my eyes. "And run into her? No. Besides, I threw away my costume." Saying it made the sugar in my stomach hurt.

He tried to reach out to me, but I brushed his hand away. I stomped past him. "You got what you wanted. You won."

Behind me, I thought I heard a sigh or muttering. I hurried up the stairs. My heart pounded, body shaking, but not from the nerves of playing the game. For once, I wasn't playing.

Audrey

The atmosphere inside *Infinity Games & Comics* changed overnight, literally overnight. Uncle Rick had gotten the call from the city manager. Mega Mart had pulled their request to rezone the strip mall. Now, he was zipping around the store straightening products and talking to customers as if he'd still have customers in the days to come.

I pulled the long receipt from the till to tally the sales from yesterday.

Uncle Rick appeared behind the counter and plucked it from my hand. "I can handle this, hun. If you wanna go home early, you can."

"I don't mind," I said.

He nodded and folded the thin strip into my palm with a smile. Under his graying beard, he almost looked like Santa with giant toothy grin.

"Good news?"

"Yeah, very. Looks like the store is safe for now, and the other stores in the strip are pooling together to update the signage. A facelift to the front will help with customer traffic, sales, and the property values for the neighborhood behind us."

I pressed the receipt between my fingers. "That's great!"

Uncle Rick kept talking like a squirrel on speed. "All the people we got to sign the petition are worried about another giant coming in and asking to take the land. They're talking about a fundraiser to beautify the entrance."

"Boo!" Dan jumped out from the stockroom door.

I screeched and hit the cabinet, rattling the breakables inside. I almost fell all the way to the floor.

Uncle Rick smacked Dan on the arm. "Stop fooling around. We have customers."

Two teenage girls snickered on the other side of the store. Dan apologized, "Sorry, Dad." He reached to help me back up, and once on my feet, I took a smack at his arm, too. Jerk.

"Hey! I said, sorry." Dan pouted as if my light tap actually hurt.

"Baby," I said.

Uncle Rick shook his head and went into the stockroom.

Reaching under the cabinet, Dan grabbed his jacket. We still had an hour until closing. Even if we'd gotten back into a groove, it didn't mean I'd let him off the hook.

"Where the heck do you think you're going?" I crossed my arms.

"I just gave Dad a good reason to get me out of the store. Besides, I need to help Sara fix her car. She said something about a banging noise when she was driving. I told her I'd take a look tonight, since she'd be at your house."

I blinked. "You know how to fix cars?" I pointed at his nose. "*You.*"

He laughed and batted my finger back down. "How do you think I get that POS truck to run at all? The thing is older than I am."

"Guess that makes sense."

Dan seemed freer, kinda like his dad. It was as if the stress had made everything more intense, and now that they could think about other things, they both returned to the people I knew. The family I loved. I held the feeling in, like a breath I couldn't let go.

He walked around the counter. "Need anything before I leave? Sara's probably waiting on me. Cars don't fix themselves."

"No, I'm cool. You go."

"Awesome." Dan hurried out the door, the jingling bells sounding happier in his wake.

Though, maybe the bells were happy for me. On my way down to Austin, I'd swing by and pick Kyle up for the con. He didn't have to protect his Dad's feelings any more, at least, not at his own expense. Now he was willing to take a chance for us to be together. One weekend. It might be a small victory, but I'd take it. I'd take any win that got Kyle a taste of real life.

Another customer came inside, jingling the bells of joy. With the same enthusiasm that possessed Uncle Rick and Dan, I smiled. "Can I help you?"

Kyle

I rolled up three more shirts into the duffel on the bed, tucked in a bag of toiletries, and packed a pair of jeans. Done already? One lone duffel was easy to fill, since Boba Fett had been carried off to the dump. I felt naked without it. The six-oh helped me make the costume, and I always had it with me. It was weird to even think about. But, I'd be going to Austin with Audrey. I needed focus on how everything was going to be right for once.

Two weeks of silent treatment had worked better than I imagined. Dad gave me space, thinking I needed to "get over" my breakup, and he didn't question anything I did. He was preoccupied with his town hall tomorrow evening, and as long as Aunt Beth covered for me like she promised, I'd have freedom for one weekend.

Only one weekend. I sighed, sat in my desk chair, and propped my head up with my elbow on the space where my laptop should be. I closed my eyes. Audrey's smile, her laugh, the sparkle in her big, brown eyes…I'd finally see her tomorrow. That must be why they called it the home *stretch*, because time dilated as the wait came to a close.

The door banged open. I clutched my chest, taking a deep breath to stop the impending heart attack.

Dad stood inside the doorway, his body tight and so without motion it felt like he'd never move. The creases by his mouth deepened, scrunching up his crow's feet and worry lines across his brow. He stared at me with wide, unrelenting eyes.

I opened my mouth, then shut it. Silent treatment. He'd have to talk first.

Against the supposed inertia keeping him rooted, he took three big steps to the bed, and I rolled the chair to get out of his way. Methodically, he unzipped the duffel and took my T-shirts and toiletries out one by one.

"What're you doing?" I said before my gut warning stopped me.

"When will you stop lying?"

My jaw hung open as I watched him empty the duffel. Aunt Beth, did she rat me out?

Dad leaned over the bed, eyes squeezed shut and lips sucked in like he was holding back tears. Was he really? Did I hurt him for real, or was it part of his act to get me to "behave?"

His words seeped out like steam. "I actually believed you, that you were going to Beth's for the weekend. What were you fixing to do this time? Run off and not come home? Another convention? What?"

"I…"

He turned to me, pain written into each line on his face. "I do everything for you, Son. Why would you do this to me?"

Do this to me? Because my need to have a life is some attack on him? It wasn't about him, but that's what he thought. He had to be acting. All this time, I was worried for his feelings, trying to keep him from missing Mom and delving back into the despair from her death. It was too long ago, and somewhere along the line, it stopped being about his feelings and more about his need for control over my life. I controlled inanimate objects. Maybe it wasn't totally normal, but I didn't hurt anyone.

"It's my life. I'll be eighteen next year, and then—"

"Then what, Kyle? What?" Dad flipped a switch, the same contorted features from the shaking of his clenched jaw instead.

I gripped the edge of the desk. "You can't run my life anymore."

"It's for your good, you ungrateful—"

"It's not!" I stood, bumping the chair so it rolled halfway across the room. "You're crazy! If Mom were alive, she'd never let you do this." I breathed harder, words breaking through the brain-filter in a rush. "She's your excuse for everything. It's been over six years. I'm done doing the eggshell thing for you."

Dad's hardened fist gripped the empty duffel, and he threw it to the floor. "Don't you dare talk about your mother like that."

"Or what? Send me to Alcatraz?" My voice shook. I was shaking, but not with nerves.

"Kyle Gene Porter."

The words exploded on their own. "You're gonna regret this."

The anger on Dad's face shifted into a mocking smile. A smile? "Oh yeah, right."

"Get out of my room!" I grabbed a shirt from the bed and chucked it at him.

He let it fall, a small sway in his bulky form. His stupid smirk wavered into an uncertain pout, only for a second. "Thought you were grounded before? You've dug your hole so deep you'll be picking dirt out of your teeth." He did a slow blink, turned, and exited the room with an extra-forceful slam to the door.

I couldn't hold my hands still, shivering from my fingers and all the way up my arms. I kicked the bedpost. My toe throbbed, and all I wanted to do was hit something. But I didn't.

Rage, depression, fear, none of it solved anything. Dad was gonna treat me like a puppet child forever unless I cut the strings. But how? The only way he'd listen to me is if he was caught being wrong.

My blood pumped harder as the anger left. I could prove him wrong, and he'd see that cosplay and the six-oh weren't childish games. All I had to do was bring the fight to his turf. The town hall tomorrow…there wasn't much time.

For the next couple hours, I didn't dare emerge from my room. Occasionally I could hear car chases or explosions from the TV downstairs. It kept on playing. Dad needed to get up for work in the morning, so why'd he still be awake this late? I could check…but if he caught me…

I shook my head. If I was gonna find a way to contact Audrey, I had to leave the bedroom eventually. Keeping my hand on the knob, I cracked open the door. Dad's bedroom was dark, so was the hall, and only the flicker from the TV lit the stairs. I tiptoed out into the hall and paused. Still no motion or other noise. *Good, maybe I'm home free.* Another few steps took me to the top of the stairs. I crouched, and it all made sense. Dad had passed out in the recliner, a six-pack empty at his feet.

Maybe I shouldn't have said that stuff about Mom. A brief pang of guilt tore at me, then shifted back into that fist-shaking anger. I descended the stairs faster, not as afraid to wake him. I passed in front of the recliner to the laptop on the coffee table. It took a minute to startup. The melodic Windows jingle stopped my heart, and I glanced back to see Dad's chest rise in the rhythm of sleep. I exhaled, and opened my messenger.

Audrey's name popped up as online.

Me: Retype phone number. I need to call you.

Her number appeared, and I ran to the phone in the kitchen to dial it before I forgot.

Audrey picked up immediately. "Are you okay?" she asked before I even said hello.

"You want truth or social convention?" I sighed and leaned my head into the doorframe between the kitchen and dining room.

"That bad," she said. "What happened?"

"Dad made me trash my costume, Aunt Beth ratted me out, and I'm on house arrest to the third power. Dad's gonna keep me home 'til Monday under surveillance."

Audrey didn't respond right away, her breaths puffing into the receiver. "We'll have to think of a way to sneak you out."

I leaned back to listen for Dad, still asleep. I whispered. "Yes, but first I have a plan. I need you to contact Josh for me. It'll be a rush, but I need you to get all the guys who are planning on going to Austin and see if they can give up Friday at the con to stop in Waco tomorrow evening."

"What? Why?"

The plan sounded crazier out loud as I detailed everything to Audrey. I had no way to make contact, so she'd have to organize everything. She could do it. Audrey could do anything.

Audrey's typing echoed over the phone line as she made notes. "Okay, got it. Leave it to me."

We whispered goodbyes, and I returned to my dark room. Everything was left in its place. Motionless. Quiet. But inside me, the light burned brighter than before. I warned Dad that I'd fight back. This time, he'd finally open his eyes to see I had an army.

Audrey

After I hung up with Kyle, I called Josh, who was more surprised at getting a call at all than the fact it was already midnight. Sane people know to text. When I told him about Kyle's costume meeting the trash can, he lost the yawn in his voice and came up with something that should cheer Kyle up. It meant one more stop for me before leaving, but it'd be worth it.

I explained Kyle's plan, then added, "But it's so late. How will we get anyone in time?"

Josh laughed. "Most of the guys in the garrison are way out of school. They've taken extra days off work, and some are already in Austin probably drinking at the hotel bar by now."

"You'll call them for me?"

"Of course." He yawned. "Also, I'll leave the box on my stoop before heading to school in the morning. Sorry I can't make it early enough myself."

I gripped the phone tight. "No, don't worry. You're doing everything you can. Thank you."

He hung up, and I sat at my desk staring at the closed blinds. I had to get to sleep. Tomorrow was going to be a long, long day. But the more I thought about how little time I had to sleep, the more awake I felt.

On the left side of the street, towering junipers flanked the front door of a house like two watchtowers just as he described it—Kyle's house. I parked a few houses down to stay out of sight. A thunderous engine roared in the distance before the monster pickup turned the corner. Kyle and his dad arrived right on time. I slid down into my seat, ducking below the dash. The doors slammed, followed by two pairs of footsteps and the front door of the house banging shut after. Settling in for the wait, I reclined the seat and got out my tablet to read. A few hours later, a door slam jolted me from the story.

Kyle's dad locked the deadbolt, and I squeezed back under the dash. The engine rattled my door as he passed, and once the truck was long gone, I ran across the street to Kyle's house.

He'd said to meet at the back door. Manicured flowerbeds curved around the perimeter, brimming with colorful shrubs, succulents, and garden statues made of glass. An adorable wooden bridge startled a cute pond in the center of an overly green lawn. The flawless landscape projected an image of a happy home—affluent, stable or something like that. What a lie.

A covered patio led to a sliding glass door at the back. Kyle sat at the kitchen table just inside, and he jumped to his feet the second he spotted me.

I reached for the handle, but he shook his head. "Alarm," he said, muffled by the glass.

He grabbed a phone from the table, took a breath, and slid the door open.

Screeeeeeeeeeeeeeeeeeeeeeeeeeeeeeeeeeeeeeeech!

Clasping my hands over my ears barely muffled the shrill noise. Strobe lights on the back of the house flashed, and I had to look down at the perfect grass. "How are you—"

The phone in Kyle's hand rang, which we somehow heard over the racket of the alarm. He answered, "Hello."

After a short pause, Kyle said, "No. Uh…no, no. Yes. Um, yeah I forgot the code." Another pause. "Cowboys. Yes, thank you."

He hung up, and seconds later the awful noise and flashing stopped. A leftover ring hung in my ears.

"You weren't kidding about house arrest." I dug my pinky into my ear to get out the stuffy feeling.

Kyle sighed as he grabbed his duffel from inside and slid the glass door into place. "Nope. But, I'm done being his prisoner. Time to do something about it."

I grabbed his hand, and we jogged to the street where my car was waiting. He went to open the passenger door, but I cut him off and opened the back seat instead.

He pouted. "Really?"

"Look."

A cardboard box sat on the seat. Kyle ducked in and opened it to see a red and black Mandalorian helmet atop the matching costume. The jumpsuit was cheaply made, some cracks in the armor plates, and of course the colors were all wrong for Boba Fett.

I peeked through the gap on the other side of the door to see his face, wide mouth and slackened cheeks. He didn't speak.

My lungs froze solid, but I managed to explain, "It's not six-oh regulation. Josh said he did his first costume in custom colors, something about the Mercs. Anyway he said you can borrow it as long…"

Kyle popped out of the car and stood in front of me still gaping like a fish. Little tears started to form along the bottoms of his eyes. Was he that disappointed? I opened my mouth to say something, but he grabbed the sides of my face and pressed his lips to mine, hard. I couldn't breathe. I didn't want to.

Once he pulled away, the wet sheen left his eyes, and he smiled. Heat flooded my cheeks. Kyle didn't blush at all, just grinned.

"You're welcome." I squeaked, then cleared my throat. "Get changed in the back seat. We don't have much time before the town hall starts."

He either couldn't speak or didn't want to spoil the moment, simply nodded and got in the car. He'd said all he needed to with that kiss.

Kyle

My elbow throbbed from banging it into the car door, and I bruised a spot on my side with the holster during the changing process. None of it mattered. Wearing the armor and helmet, I was whole again. Audrey seemed to understand. The whole ride through town, her grin reflected in the rearview mirror.

We pulled into the parking lot and my chest tightened. Josh's costume fit right, so it wasn't that. Was I really going to speak up in the town hall? People were supposed to take the mic and ask questions at these events. It'd be okay. My photo-op stunt would help him, not hurt. He'd see. He'd understand.

Historical evidence didn't support that idea, but that was the point. Something had to change.

I got out of the car, Audrey by my side. A large circular fountain was positioned in the center right outside the city hall, the ground covered in tan bricks that blended into the walls of the main building. Unoffending beige stretched as far as the eye could see. But off to the right of the fountain, a clone trooper, two stormtroopers, an imperial guard, and one Darth Vader were erecting a space backdrop for photography. The black canvas speckled with stars and planets stood apart from everything else.

One of the stormtroopers set his helmet down and grabbed a long box from the ground. "Hey, give me a hand?" He nodded at me. It was Mike, the garrison leader. He had seen the original trilogy in theaters, lucky guy.

"Sure." I jogged over and took hold of the other end of the box, holding on so he could slide out the rolled-up sign. "Thanks for coming. You don't know how much this means to me."

"What was that?"

Right, the helmet. I took it off as well. "I said, I can't thank you enough for coming back after you were already in Austin."

Mike clicked two metal poles together and popped it into the base. "No, Kyle, thank you. We've probably bled the con attendees in Texas dry by now. Public events like this, awesome idea."

Wasn't Mike one of the guys who got those asshat cosplayers thrown out of the con before? He didn't know I was involved in that drama at all. Mike was just one of those guys who liked helping people, especially the Magic Makers foundation.

Together we unrolled the charity's banner. Audrey assisted, and we hung it next to the backdrop. Bright flowers surrounded a bald kid smiling in a sparkly princess dress, which juxtaposed the dark space scene. The connection was obvious—fantasy. Wonder.

A couple of cars drove into the passenger drop-off loop next to the parking lot. Six more six-oh members got out while the drivers went to find a place to park. Various imperial costumes, more troopers, and a few guards were among the newcomers. That made eleven, twelve, thirteen people.

"That's a lot to make it on short notice." The courtyard began to look like the lobby at a small con. It was more than I could have hoped.

Mike smacked my back. The stiff armor knocked the wind out of me. "Just wait. Josh called in the cavalry." He laughed.

Did he actually wink? I moved to ask, but he left to organize the group into standing positions. Acting as garrison leader gave a chance for his military background to shine through.

Our Darth pointed to the other side of the fountain. A crowd had gathered, wondering what we were up to. "Show time, guys."

Audrey stood behind the camera on the tripod and waved at the people. "Don't be shy. We're ready for you!"

Curious pedestrians and city employees began to wander to our side. I put on my helmet, found my place beside my brothers, and posed with the public. The donation bucket began to fill. Some wandered into the building for the town hall in session.

As we took pictures, car after car drove through the drop off. Others parked, filling up the city hall's lot, and stormtroopers appeared in the courtyard from all directions. Three here, ten there, and more six-oh members than I could catch while taking photos. Wait, was that a Jedi? A handful of Jedi and a couple of other Rebel characters walked past.

"Excuse me." I nodded to Audrey and slipped away from the backdrop. Another Boba Fett seamlessly took my place.

Waves of white, black, and dots of red costumes concealed the previous sea of beige bricks. Mike organized the troopers into lines, and they marched back and forth for the growing crowd. Some of the Jedi performed mock battles with the Imperials, and people from nearby buildings came to see all the fuss. There had to be fifty cosplayers at least. The guys from Fort Worth even brought the remote-controlled droids and had them out for kids to take turns steering.

"Formation A!" Mike called. The storm and clone troopers formed a triangle, followed by loud applause.

I tapped his shoulder armor. "How'd you get so many to come?"

"Check Audrey's phone." Mike faced his squad of troopers again. "And march!"

I hurried to the camera and waited for her to pause taking photos between customers. "Let me see your phone, please."

"Sure."

She fished it out of her pocket, and the lock screen showed four unread texts from Josh.

Mission Accomplished.

Tell Kyle sorry for me. I'll see him in Austin tomorrow.

I got all the guys from Dallas, Fort Worth, and most of the small towners nearby.

The Rebels wanted in on the action, too. Take a pic of the crowd :-D

Audrey finished another set of pictures and took the phone back, checking the screen. "Don't you need to go in? The meeting should be ending soon."

My pulse quickened. Photo ops fell safely within my comfort zone, and I was about to leap out of it. More than that, I thought a handful of hardcore guys would show. I had no idea Josh and Mike could pull off a miracle. Maybe that's what this was, a miracle, both for me and for the kids that Magic Makers served. The donation bucket had already been emptied once, and that didn't account for all the donations through credit card.

"Right." I squeezed her hand, then found a couple of troopers among the forming battalion. "Hey, can you two come with me? I need to announce our fundraiser to the people inside. The town hall should be just about finished."

Behind Audrey, more cosplayers seemed to appear out of nowhere, so many that I could hardly see the regular people waiting in line behind a flood of Jedi and Imperials. Audrey patted my shoulder and returned to taking picture after picture, doing her job. I had to do mine.

With the troopers at my sides, we marched into Waco City Hall. The clerk at the reception desk chuckled and waved her coworker over to get a glimpse of us. People in the hallways gave us thumbs up. The churning nerves in my stomach firmed into conviction, and underneath the helmet, I smiled.

We approached the doors to the meeting room. The troopers each grabbed a door, opening them simultaneously for effect. The people inside would see my red and black armor with two white troopers on either side. Unconventional uniforms in a place of politics and serious business. Maybe that gave us more real authority. After all, I came here to make a difference…to make a change.

I walked into the lecture hall. One long aisle split the room, separating two sections of chairs. Someone was standing behind a microphone halfway down the aisle, and at the front stood a carpeted stage.

At the podium, Dad's mouth parted as the color drained from his face. He continued speaking, like he couldn't stop if he wanted to. "And…uh…yes, school funding. Yes. I fully back the bond package going up for a vote in a few months."

Dad adjusted his cowboy hat and tried desperately to look anywhere but at the three costumed freaks. "We're almost out of time. Any other questions?"

All the pretend strength I used in JROTC to stand at attention and march became something real. Solid. I removed my helmet and held it in the crook of my arm, shoulders straight. "I just wanted to thank my Dad for the opportunity to come here this evening. I have a quick announcement."

Still as concrete, Dad retained a neutral smile. He looked normal to the audience, but underneath the statue stance, Dad had to be holding his rage like a Coke in the trunk on a summer day.

I made eye contact, trying to convey *It's okay. Just wait,* but we didn't have that kind of connection. He stared back. I couldn't read him either.

This was it. Squeezing the helmet, I lifted my chin. "I represent the Six Hundred and Second Battalion, a costuming organization, and we're out front doing photos for charity. All donations go to the Magic Makers Foundation which benefits sick and disabled children around the nation."

Dad's pale complexion heated a few percentage points in the red direction. "I didn't—"

"That's awesome. Can I get a picture?" A woman asked from the seat next to me.

"Yes, just outside."

"Who'd have thought to do a fundraiser like that," said another man.

I faced the mic once more. "Thank you again, Mr. Porter, for sharing your spotlight with our group."

The audience applauded, the sound lifting me up. Weightless. As the troopers and I marched down the aisle, I floated through space like an astronaut on the ISS. Nothing could bring me down.

When we reached the doors, Dad announced, "That concludes this town hall. Thank y'all for stopping in."

Bright sun blinded me as we exited the building, and the audience followed behind. Gasps and shouts of surprise came from all around. My eyes adjusted to the spectacle of marching stormtroopers, squads of imperial officers acting for the crowd, whirring droids zipping about, and the photo booth with a line past the fountain. More people had arrived, probably to see what the commotion was all about. The once-serene plaza had exploded into a convention-sized crowd of cosplayers with bodies packed together, the sounds of conversation rising to a low roar.

They had all rallied here for me, for the six-oh, and for the charity. Soon Dad would see everyone in costume on the doorstep of his world. I didn't expect this turnout. He might've overlooked a couple of us, but this?

Hammering heartbeats fired into hyperventilating lungs, but I couldn't stop smiling, like a lunatic walking the green mile. Would Dad come talk to me now, or wait 'til we got home? Would he stop me from going to Austin? Was he livid, was he happy, or would he let the unknown kill me before he left city hall.

The last option, for sure.

I stepped off the walkway into the grass to make room for the people pouring out of the building.

Dad crossed the threshold, and the whites around his pupils seemed to grow, like the eyes themselves couldn't take in any more of the crazy. After he surveyed the entirety of the courtyard, Dad's gaze landed on me, and he started walking.

A few people from the town hall audience stopped him halfway.

"Oh, Mr. Porter. What an excellent idea to invite them to the town hall." A man in a Cowboys tie shook Dad's hand.

The woman next to him said, "I love Magic Makers, and so creative to have *Star Wars* characters. Look at this, it's like a carnival! I wish I had brought my daughter."

Numerous people shook his hand and parted the way for him. One added, "You should advertise the charity event beforehand next time."

Dad stuttered, "Yes. Yes of course. Thank you."

He shook a few more hands, smiled his diplomatic smile, and managed to break through the mob to where I stood in the grass. He was breathing quickly, and his red face had turned kind of purple. He hadn't said anything yet, just waited there glancing around at the courtyard filled with shiny white plastic and laughter.

Fine. If I had to speak first, I would. "What do you think? Cosplay is just childish kids' stuff, huh?" It came out snarkier than I meant.

"Yeah."

The one word answer dropkicked the air out of my chest. "But—"

"But what? That you orchestrated this circus to humiliate me? That you made damn sure my voters know I'm a part a your damn fashion show?

But *what*, Son?" Beads of sweat dripped from under his hat, anger into actual heat.

This wasn't how it was supposed to go. Dad was supposed to see things like I did. He was supposed to understand. My rebellion, my courage, my victory…it all congealed into lead, dropping my stomach into my borrowed boots.

My numb fingers couldn't keep a grip on the helmet, and it plopped onto the grass. "I wanted to show you that there's more to it than a costume, but…"

"Kyle!" Audrey yelled.

I turned, and she was walking our way with a woman in a skirt suit and a cameraman. Holy crap, did someone call the news? It was Maria Briggs, the community interest reporter.

That's just what I needed, that and to throw up. Looked like Dad felt the same, though the politician in him covered it all with a well-prepared smile.

Audrey got to us first and started introductions. "And here they are. Kyle and his dad organized the event."

I nodded, teeth bared or flashing a grin. Both really. "Hi." I leaned over Audrey's shoulder and whispered, "Did you call them?"

She shook her head and stepped out of the way as the reporter waved the camera guy to the side. A sudden applause from the crowd interrupted us, so we had to wait for the lull. Someone probably won a droid race or maybe they added a raffle.

Maria Briggs tapped her overly hair-sprayed bob. "I'd love to do a short interview with you two. It'll be just a few questions. Is that okay?"

Dad gave her a firm handshake. "Yes, Ma'am. We'd love to."

She smiled, white teeth and bright red lipstick. "Thank y'all so much." Turning to the camera, she counted down on her fingers, then spoke into the microphone. "I'm here with City Council Member Cole Porter and his son, Kyle. This is quite the charity event. How'd you come up with the idea?" She pointed he mic at Dad.

Dad looked at her then the camera, and turned on the charm. Free publicity worked like magic. "I've been wanting to do something big for the city. I have to thank Kyle though. He's the one in the costume group, and they regularly hold events like this."

"Is that so?" Maria held the mic under my nose. "Tell us about what's happening here today?"

With the black lens of the camera staring at me like an eye, and the microphone shoved close to my face, I couldn't think. Dad smiled at me. It all seemed so surreal, and I kind of watched myself from far away. I bantered on about the six-oh and charity and the spiel that I'd heard Mike, Josh, and a lot of the other members say over and over. Dad popped in here and there, taking credit where he could while trying to look "cool." We paused the interview a couple minutes to move a few more feet away from the ruckus in the plaza.

"So this is a nationwide organization then? How'd you get involved locally?" She asked.

I didn't think. My mouth just answered, "I got into cosplay and the six-oh years ago, and Dad's supported me from day one. He stood by my side, and I wanted to give back, both to him and the charity. I thought hosting the fundraiser here would do both."

The image I had of him just then, smiling and being with me in costume, I could pretend it was real. I took a snapshot in my head and captured a memory to hold onto.

It was all I ever wanted.

"So kind of you. Thank you both for everything you do." Maria signaled the cameraman to turn it off. She put the mic down at her side. "Thanks, y'all. This'll air tomorrow on the community spotlight. Hope you like it!" She waved and walked away.

Dad watched her disappear into the crowd, and Audrey found her place at my side. I returned to my body, the surreal feeling passing, which let the horrible unease grip me tight all over.

"Why'd you say all that?" Dad asked, still watching the cosplayers and constituents mingle.

"What?"

He shook his head and finally looked at me. "That stuff about being by you…"

"Because I wanted it to be true," I said.

Taking off his hat, Dad wiped his forehead with his other free hand. The politician smile was gone, and yet, the blood-boiling anger hadn't surfaced. He chewed his lip, watching me and Audrey. If I could have any superpower, magic, or hyper-advanced tech, I'd pick telepathy just to know what he was thinking.

Someone smacked my shoulder armor. "Hey, kiddo. Why didn't you tell me Cole Porter was your old man?" Still in full stormtrooper armor, Mike laughed and reached out to shake Dad's hand, but he didn't accept it. "Shit man, it's been ages."

Dad cocked his head. "Who're you?"

Mike removed the helmet, wiping the sweaty gray hair away from his face. "Don't remember me, Porter?"

"Boom Mike? Holy crap, how long has it been?" Dad gripped his arm and shook in a smooth motion, practiced and perfect.

"Don't think I've seen you since discharge, and I've been just up in Fort Worth. If I'd have known you were so close, man." He set his helmet and prop blaster on the grass.

Dad laughed, an honest and full laugh. "I've got a law office in the city."

When was the last time I saw him raw and happy? Forever, years…I couldn't remember.

"That nails it. We're getting drinks next week." Mike rested his elbow on my shoulder, the plastic squeaking as it rubbed. "You must be proud of this kid here. I don't see many his age work so hard for other people."

Dad bobbed his head. "Yeah. That's, um…yeah. So you do this costume group too then, huh?"

Mike folded his arms, a large breath raising the breastplate. "I came across the six-oh-second through Magic Makers actually. A few years ago, my daughter Ella got picked for one of their wish-come-true vacations. She's in remission now, but it was a scary time."

"I'm so sorry…" Dad seemed to shrink a little.

"We're past it. We survived, and now we give back. At first, thought the six-oh was just for fanboys who wanted to live in the movies, but they're so much more." He chuckled. "It's fun, and I can teach these guys how to march like a real Marine."

Dad snorted. "JROTC does that, too."

"And we can cast a wider net. You should look into the six-oh yourself. I can get a costume done up. Father-son duo." Mike elbowed me in the arm.

Dad nodded politely. "Heh, no thanks. I'll see you next week then?"

"You bet." Mike picked up his helmet and blaster from the ground. "Gotta talk to the guys who are continuing on to Austin tonight. See you there?"

I looked at Dad. "Will he?"

Dad did that half-nod head bobbing thing again. "Yeah, uh. Sure."

Mike pivoted and marched back into the fray, followed by chanting as his squad began another routine.

I was left behind with Dad who looked even more lost than before. Mouth slack and eyes glazed as his gaze went over my shoulder. Laughter, shouts, and the buzz of excitement covered our silence.

Audrey pressed next to my side, like a pillar of support. Without speaking, just her presence seemed to say *"Don't give up. Look at him."* Or maybe those were my own thoughts. It was hard to tell.

I chewed my cheek. "I didn't want to embarrass you. I just wanted you to see cosplay like I did. I thought it'd help you, really."

A moment passed, and he didn't reply, pressing his lips flat and furrowing his brow. Audrey squeezed my hand. Finally Dad exhaled. "I won't promise to like any of this stuff. I can't. But, I know when to fold 'em. I'll try to listen more."

I opened my mouth, but there was nothing to fight. Nothing to yell back about. He wanted to try and meet me halfway, and that was more than I'd hoped. A sudden breathlessness choked me, like I was about to cry, but I couldn't. I just smiled that grinning idiot smile. "Really?"

"Really."

I blurted, "Can I really go to Austin?"

"Boom Mike would wonder where you were. I said you could, and *I* keep my promises." His tone shifted some at the end.

Coming here was the right thing to do, but I did lie. I did break promises. Dad made me defend myself, but that wasn't how I wanted to keep living. We didn't need to fight a cold war. Not anymore. "I'm sorry."

"Thank you, Son. You're still grounded when you get home on Sunday."

"Yes, Sir." I saluted, unironically this time.

It had been hanging in the back of my mind, and Dad seemed to be reasonable, so I dared. "What about boot camp?"

He frowned and nodded. "We'll discuss it, but I know you don't want to go. Maybe there's a weekend one or somethin'."

I wanted to hug him without worrying like I had as a kid, but I couldn't move my feet. I settled for a smile. "Thanks, Dad."

Dad reached out and laid a hand on my shoulder. Not a hug, but he tried. We tried. He glanced at Audrey, who squeezed my hand. "Young lady."

She nodded.

An almost smile formed on his lips. "I'm sure I'll see more of you in the future."

Audrey twisted her sneaker on the grass for a minute. "Okay, Mr. Porter."

The sounds from the crowd seemed to get louder even as a lot of the people began to get in cars and leave. The commotion gave some distraction from the strained quiet between the three of us. Maybe I hadn't forced some earth-shattering understanding or a miracle reconnection with Dad, but it was a start. We both dropped our weapons and dared to try another perspective. I'd say a lot of people never make it that far.

The three of us completed an awkward goodbye, and Audrey and I caravanned the rest of the way to Austin behind Mike and the others. For the first time, I had real permission to go to a con. It felt like peace to me.

30

Audrey

The adrenaline from the town hall carried Kyle and me through Saturday at the con, but we decided to leave early Sunday morning to get home. I had spent so many weekends away. For some reason, I needed to be with my own family.

Noontime sun brightened the foyer in a way I rarely got to see. The open floor plan let in the light. During all my evenings at home, I hadn't really noticed. The warmth of real light filled me like air.

In the kitchen, Mom was rinsing the blender from her smoothie, and the TV in the living room jumped from channel to channel. Dad sat in the recliner with the remote.

I yawned and flopped onto the sofa.

Dad flicked past another golf game. "I can put on something you want, if you'd like."

"Nawh, I'll watch whatever."

"I'm using the washing machine," Sara called from the back door. She made a ruckus with the washer, shut it, and it began to whir. A minute later, she entered the living room and stopped. "Hey, stranger. Aren't you supposed to be in Austin?"

My jaw popped in another yawn. "I came home early."

Dad let the TV rest on a newscast. "I told you not to let Rick run you ragged. I heard you haven't even been paid for all that work."

"It's okay. They need it more than me right now." I twisted forward to set my feet on the floor. "That's not why left this morning."

"Yeah?" Sara took a seat beside me.

Mom leaned over the granite counter that divided the rooms. "It rained yesterday, so you've got the lawn to mow again. I'm pretty sure the hamper is full, too."

I groaned. "I know, but I was hoping to have a break."

"You should've thought about that before." Mom's tone sounded playful, though underneath she probably meant it.

Dad set his footrest down and looked around the room at each of us. He switched off the TV. "All my girls at home."

"That's the point," I said. "I don't have money to pay for everyone, but I wanted to go to the movies together. We could get dinner, too, maybe. I know Mom's probably got papers to grade, or there's something Dad wants to watch."

"Stop right there." Mom walked around the counter into the living room with us. "Let's do it."

Sara stood, looking down at me. "You need to get dressed."

I laughed and hurried upstairs to change. The movie we saw that day was, well, we didn't walk out so it couldn't have been that bad. But we tore the plot to pieces over sushi right afterward. Dad had sprung for the deluxe platter, which came with the salmon roe pieces. I dared Sara to eat the orange balls. She'd gagged and had to spit it in a cloth napkin. I hadn't laughed so hard in ages.

We could've let that outing be one shining moment against the bustle of the everyday. How we all had our own lives and interests, jobs, homework, and excuses. But I was done being all about me. Now, it was all about us.

Four Months Later

The bells jingled again. I never thought I'd get tired of hearing them, but I kinda wanted to take them off the door. Customers mingled near the wall 'o comics, yakking about the latest series, and a few others sat on new chairs upholstered in comic fabric. We had added a conversation corner in the back, which allowed people to linger or make the shop a meeting place before games or conventions. That one was Dan's idea.

At the register, I rang up a couple of purchases for one of our new regulars. He carried his boarded and bagged new releases out the door, which jingled yet again.

Uncle Rick finished stocking the anime merchandise and joined me behind the counter. "How are the sales from the website this week?"

"Up three percent. The banner ads on the ConHub have a good click-through rate. I think it's helping. At least sixty percent of the new purchases used the promotion code." I opened the analytics tab on the computer next to the register that he finally let me put in.

He gave me a side hug. "I'm sorry I didn't listen to you before about making changes. You and Dan."

"I'm happy they're working out."

The bells jingled; Dan waltzed straight to the register. He leaned over the glass case and tapped me on the shoulder. "Tag. You can head on home."

Uncle Rick chuckled. "I'll be doing inventory."

Once he disappeared behind the curtain, Dan put his hand on the case and vaulted into the spot beside me. "Don't you have plans with Kyle tonight?"

"Yes, but I need to show you how to do the new coupon thing on the register."

He shoved me aside with his hip. "I can figure it out."

"Like you figured out the last one? No thanks." I nudged him, too, and he hopped sideways like I'd pushed him hard. "Dork."

"Takes one to know one." He made a fart noise with his lips.

Yeah, real mature.

"Are you two done being eight-year-olds?" Sara appeared in front of the register. I hadn't even heard the bells since they'd rung so many times.

"Never!" Dan smacked the glass. He shook his reddening hand. "Ow."

I wiped a rag over his palm print. "Serves you right."

Straightening her body, Sara slid her hand down the strap on her purse. "Anyone here gonna help a customer? I need advice for something to decorate my dorm room."

Dan zipped to the other side of the counter. "I'm on duty to help you, Miss."

"Fine, I'm outta here then. I've got a hot date." I wiped the case with one last swipe and walked around the counter like a normal human, instead of whatever hyper elf that possessed Dan.

"See ya later." Dan smiled.

"Later." I walked toward the door and glanced back.

Dan and Sara were getting cozy by the wall scroll box. I couldn't help but grin. Looks like I wasn't the only one with a date tonight.

Kyle
Also Four Months Later

I came out of the hotel bathroom wearing Josh's custom Mando armor again. Dad was sitting at the tiny desk near the window, typing away on his laptop.

"I was gonna hit the dealers' room and see Audrey before heading to the alternate history panel. Did you want to come?" I poured water into the top of the coffee maker and turned it on.

Dad shook his head. "I agreed to come with you so I could meet a client. I'm working this weekend."

The coffee machine sputtered and hissed. "Just thought since we were here."

He glanced up from the screen and looked down again. "Ain't my show, you know that."

"I know." The noises stopped, and I grabbed the foam cup, which I could hardly feel in my glove. I set it next to Dad's computer.

"Thank you, Son." He smiled. For real smiled.

"No problem."

Dad took a sip as he inspected my gloves, the cheaply painted armor, and finally my face. He still smiled, but his eyes seemed heavy. "Your mom really loved this stuff, didn't she."

"Yeah." Talking about her out loud after so long stung a little, but afterward it felt good, like maybe we should've been doing it all along.

He returned to typing. "Don't care for all this stuff, but I'll see the show you're in tonight."

"Really?"

Dad nodded. "Now go on. Your girlfriend is waitin' for you."

At the mention of Audrey, the weight of our conversation lifted. I had a whole weekend to spend with her. We didn't get to see each other often because of school, work, and the whole living-over-an-hour-away thing. But when a con came around, we owned it—together.

THE END

Acknowledgements

First of all, I must thank my outstanding husband for giving me the opportunity to go to critique groups, sell books at conventions, and for his unending support in all things writing and life. I love you, sweetheart. I also thank my amazing daughter, who inspires me with her own fathomless creativity and spark.

I'll give a big thank you as always to my mom for being the best cheerleader, and another huge thanks for the enthusiastic support from my mother in law, Beth, and father in law, Gene. To my sisters in law, I hope you like this book too! I love writing stuff for you guys.

I can't bow down and thank Jane enough for reading SO MANY versions of this book, and thank you Heather for your amazing talent in editing to make it shine. I'd like to thank Alex, Laurie, Ben, Annie, Sam, and the whole crew at Denton Writers for workshopping this book into submission. For those who did full beta reads too, I love you guys. Thank you!

To my word wizard, Tex, arigatou! Thank you for the beta, the feedback, and for making me pick myself back up when I was down. This book is only out here because of you.

Thanks again to Kara for more industry insight for this novel, too. I owe a lot to the North Texas Speculative Fiction Workshop, especially Alley, for supporting my career. I owe a lot to the DFW Writers' Conference for the connections and opportunities.

Finally, thank you to Keely, Amy S., Amy B., Louis, Diane, and every fun geeky person I know! You guys are the heart of this story. Thank you North Texas Cosplay for the inspiration and for the fun meetups. You keep this fandom fresh. And to everyone, May the Force be with you. ☺

Note from the Author

I hope you enjoyed COSPLAYED and all the geeky goodies included. Cosplay is a passion of mine, as is writing, and I'm so thankful I got to combine them both. If you enjoyed this story, please write a short review on Amazon or Goodreads. Every review helps out, and once again, thank you for reading!

Thank you ☺

About the Author

Laura is the author of the young adult fantasy series Illirin (SCHISM and UNITY) and the YA geeky romance COSPLAYED. She has an MA in Technical writing and is a Senior Editor at Anaiah Press for their YA/NA Christian Fiction.

Her gamer husband and amazing daughter give support and inspiration every day. Their cats, Talyn and Moya, provide entertainment through living room battles and phantom-dust-mote hunting. Somehow, they all manage to survive living in Texas where it is hotter than any human being should have to endure. You can find updates about writing and the random stuff in her life on her blog www.LauraMaisano.blogspot.com or follow her on twitter @MaisanoLaura. If you're more interested in just the professional angle, check out her website www.RayhaStudios.com.